BATHED IN PRAYER

MITFORD BOOKS BY JAN KARON

At Home in Mitford

A Light in the Window

These High, Green Hills

Out to Canaan

A New Song

A Common Life

In This Mountain

Shepherds Abiding

Light from Heaven

Home to Holly Springs

In the Company of Others

Somewhere Safe
with Somebody Good

Come Rain or Come Shine

To Be Where You Are

Esther's Gift:
A Mitford Christmas Story

The Mitford Snowmen

Jan Karon's Mitford
Cookbook & Kitchen Reader:
*Recipes from Mitford Cooks,
Favorite Tales from Mitford Books*

The Mitford Bedside Companion:
*New Essays, Family Photographs,
Favorite Mitford Scenes, and Much
More*

FATHER TIM'S COLLECTED QUOTES

Patches of Godlight:
Father Tim's Favorite Quotes

A Continual Feast:
*Words of Comfort and
Celebration, Collected
by Father Tim*

CHILDREN'S BOOKS BY JAN KARON

Jeremy:
The Tale of an Honest Bunny

Miss Fannie's Hat

The Trellis and the Seed:
*A Book of Encouragement
for All Ages*

JAN KARON

BATHED IN PRAYER

G. P. Putnam's Sons
New York

PUTNAM

G. P. Putnam's Sons
Publishers Since 1838
An imprint of Penguin Random House LLC
375 Hudson Street
New York, New York 10014

ISBN 9780525537564

Printed in the United States of America
1   3   5   7   9   10   8   6   4   2

Book design by Spring Hoteling

For my readers
with gratitude

BATHED
IN PRAYER

AT THE AGE OF TEN, I WROTE MY FIRST NOVEL.

The news that I would become an author was given to me as a kind of epiphany. I recall where I was standing and how I felt when this stunning forecast was made known, rather quietly, to my heart.

As an avid reader since the age of five, I spared no time; I went right to work in a perfect daze of bliss.

I set it during the run-up to the Civil War, of which I knew nothing beyond the pages of *Gone with the Wind*, recently read—literally undercover, with a flashlight. My grandfather did not believe in the dubious influence of books, especially very large books, upon the innocent minds of children.*

During this fertile period, I also saw the movie. Imagine the impact of those two fierce works in the life of a shy and dangerously curious country child. I say 'dangerous' because I was told with authority that 'curiosity killed the cat,' and I expected to die several times during any given day.

This thrilling phase of my writing career came to a bitter, but ultimately satisfying, end. My grandmother learned that my blue-lined pages contained the word famously used by Rhett Butler in the final scene of *Gone with the Wind*. Her good and proper thrashing is but one reason there's no cussin' in any of my work.

---

* For lovers of extreme trivia, my novel ran to a whopping fourteen pages, trailing behind Jane Austen's *The History of England*, a burlesque of thirty-four pages written when she was fifteen.

Do what made you happy when you were ten years old.

—Unknown

There were years when I had no clue about why I was born. I really, really wanted to discover that answer. I could hardly bear the dark knowing that I might perish without learning what I was born to do. I whined a lot to the one I perceived as a distant and disinterested God. Yes, my grandmother was a believer; she read the Bible to my little sister, Brenda, and to me, and yes, we prayed at mealtime and we certainly went to church with Shirley Temple bows in our hair and put our pennies in the offering plate and got the occasional gold star in Sunday school, but . . .

As a child, I knew that something was terribly missing. Something more than my longed-for parents. Something more than laughter in a querulous and deprecatory household.

Sometimes I was close to giving it a name; what was missing was on the proverbial tip of my tongue. But it always eluded me, refusing to be named. Decades later, I would identify the emptiness as *Pascal's hole* or his *God-shaped vacuum*.

'There is a God-shaped vacuum in the heart of every person,' wrote Blaise Pascal, a seventeenth-century physicist, mathematician, writer, and theologian, 'and it can't be filled by any created thing. It can only be filled by God, made known through Jesus Christ.'

At the age of eighteen, I was a young mother plying a trade also plied, though unknown to me, by Salman Rushdie, Joseph Heller, Ted Geisel,* Clive Cussler, James Patterson, Danielle Steel, Mary

---

* Ted Geisel was later known as Doctor Seuss.

Higgins Clark, and Gabriel García Márquez, to name but a few fiction writers who worked in advertising. I found that ad writing unleashed in me a flood of creative energies, but nothing filled the vacuum. Not the awards, not the money, though occasionally the success of a great campaign helped.

I wasted the emotional vitality of many years trying to plumb the wisdom I craved. Or maybe those years weren't wasted. Rich with longing, unknowing, and feelings ripe with the sense of loss, perhaps they were like the pitch-dark places of the Earth's mantle where diamonds are formed.

I have a great esteem for sorrow and suffering, which is easy to say for one who never endured holocaust or famine or plague or even an IRS audit. But the portion I have known convinces me that dark places can not only produce diamonds but act as the kiln from which useful vessels come forth.

All of which gives special credence to these words of St. Paul: 'In everything, give thanks.'

As someone once said: 'Do what made you happy when you were ten years old.' What had made me happy, I finally realized, was writing a book. But this was a very inconvenient truth.

The writers I read were often known to be penniless—like Poe and Keats and O'Henry and Kafka and even Thoreau, for Pete's sake, and while we're at it, look at Van Gogh.

Come boldly to the throne of grace.

—Hebrews 4:16

During what some would call midlife, I came to the end of myself.

I did what can be frightening even to contemplate—I surrendered my life. To the tenderness, mercy, and grace of the One Who loved us first.

Some of us can take just so much of our own ego, our own messiness and pride and bitterness. At some point, we want to lay it down. Turn it over. Give it up. Die to ourselves. I had wanted this forever, but here's the rub: Timing. Really. Is. Everything.

After an especially difficult circumstance in my brief history as a TV producer, I knew it was time. Just as you know when a book you're writing is ready to begin and when it's ready to end.

I got down on my knees and prayed and wept for hours. All that stuff stored in there, the good, the bad, and the ugly, came pouring out—it was my personal tsunami. I asked for forgiveness, I gave thanks for His love and for His son who is All Love. I essentially turned in my old life and asked for a new life—the one He had designed for me from the beginning. I was forty-two.

There's an early ad slogan I always liked; I think it was for a California wine. 'Nothing good happens fast.'

My walk as a new Christian was full of wonder and more than a few miracles. But it took what seemed a long, long time to gather the courage to step out on faith and do what needed to be done. I prayed with focus and kept a journal for two years, devoted strictly to how I might leave my career and write fiction. How was I to do it? How could it possibly make sense?

At the age of forty-eight, I got the green light.

Go and don't look back. I am with you. That was the message posted to my heart.

I put a For Sale sign in the front yard. The house sold in two days.

I moved to the mountains of North Carolina and sat down at a secondhand computer, knowing nothing about how to use it. So began a novel about a woman who moves to the mountains and opens an inn. But the idea didn't work. The characters didn't engage me; they remained as flat as the page. I knew something was deeply flawed, but I didn't know what.

This was the dark place that one hopes will form the diamond, the kind of place Paul asks us to give thanks for.

Readers often wonder why there are so many references to food in my early work. It was because I was writing hungry. Which can be a pretty good way to write, all things considered. Then I had a profound insight that we could easily call life-changing:

I had not surrendered my *work* to God.

I had prayed for years about stepping out on faith and writing a book, and now I had done it and I just assumed that everything was covered. You old-time Christians out there, remember I was a newly hatched chick. While I thought this was the mountaintop, God still had me in the valley. Which was a good thing. Because, like Linus with his blanket, I had my mantra:

Keep going, don't look back. I am with you.

I remember the night I was given a vision about my life's work.

I saw in my imagination a man walking down a village street. His back was to me. I had no idea he was a priest until he turned around and I saw his collar.

To tell you the truth, the 'vision' didn't look like much to me, but I knew this simple reveal was pivotal. I got out of bed immediately and started writing.

'He left the coffee-scented warmth of the Main Street Grill and stood for a moment under the green awning.'

Where would he go? What would he do?

The answer was a blank page.

Then I let him do what some of us do when we're figuring out who we are—he walked. He took notice of the mountain chill in the air. He reminded himself that it helped to be aware of the little things in life. And in those opening moments, he set a tone for the book by deciding to 'amble' and not hurry as was his wont. In a few short paragraphs, here were valuable clues to a character with whom I would spend nearly twenty-five years.

I didn't know his name for many weeks. I used the pronoun 'he' and prayed for the name that would be completely authentic.

In my clueless, I-have-never-done-this-before way, I thought it would be grand if he were Irish, as am I, on his paternal side. Deciding on the name Kavanagh (not spelled Cavanaugh or Kavanaugh, *please*) took weeks. Timothy came to me around the same time, and much later, his middle name, Andrew.

Then I needed to know where he was born. All I knew is that he was Southern. I spread a map of the United States on the floor of my writing room—interesting that I remember these small details as if they were epiphanies—and got down on my hands and knees like a child and poured over the Southern states.

He was definitely not from Tennessee, not from Georgia, not even from North Carolina, where he was the rector of the Chapel of Our Lord and Savior Jesus Christ, aka the Lord's Chapel.

How did I know he wasn't from, say, Florida or Texas? By the best barometer of all—gut. All that was left was Mississippi, and that was precisely, absolutely where he was from, though mostly what I knew of Mississippi was this: MIdoubleSIdoubleSIPPI. In grade school, I loved writing the name of this state without lifting the pencil from the page.

So I started reading (and rereading) Mississippi writers, just as he would have done, and peering into their culture, which is, in my humble opinion, more romantic, even exotic, than many other Southern states. Mississippi, they say, exists 'behind the Magnolia Curtain.' It's where classic Southern literature has always lived, or at least has a second home.

I had always been interested in the Church as a body. On a sort of casserole level, not a political level. Which is a good thing. Because I wanted to view the life of a single church and its people in a simpler way, the way most of us see it. I had been through a few major conflicts of the Church and didn't need to chew on this bitter root in my work.

I wanted to examine the struggles that come into the daily life of a working priest, the critical human stuff, like what to do with a thrown-away boy named Dooley and how to handle a heart so long devoted to his parish that it feared a loving devotion to one parishioner. How would Father Tim deal with a man who was treating his God-shaped vacuum as a toxic landfill? And when was the priest going to finally pastor himself and settle the old debts of his youth? Above all, how does one go about collecting five abandoned children, scattered like kittens from a basket, into a healing family?

Further, just as one might run to a church or monastery or convent for safety, I chose to give my readers a refuge. In Mitford, a reader may find sorrow and disappointment, sickness and loss, but there will always be connection and community, a safe place to run.

A lot of readers wonder if Mitford is real. In truth, Mitford is everywhere. You can even find it in the heart of darkness. But we must do our part. We must give a hand; we must learn to console and uplift and encourage and be courageous. Bottom line, we simply cannot wait for others to reach out. We must reach in.

> 'Whatever you can do or dream you can do,
> begin it. Boldness has genius, power, and magic
> in it.'
>
> —Misattributed to Goethe,
> believed to be from W. H. Murray

When I began writing the series at the age of fifty, I can't say I was crazy about Father Tim.

But I grew to like him very much. And what's not to like, really? He's a rosarian. A terrific cook. An avid reader. And though he's rarely called upon to do it, he can still recite much of St. Paul's letters to St. Timothy, learned as a child through the admirable habit of memorization.

Agatha Christie wrote thirty-three novels, sixty-five short stories, and one play in which a Belgian detective, Hercule Poirot, appeared. In an interview toward the end of her life, she said, 'I never really cared for that little man.'

I have cared a lot for Father Tim and for his many prayers and consolations not only to parishioners but to me. He drove me to prayer of my own when the time came for him to preach and I was the one to write the sermon, or when he needed to pray in a critical situation and I had to configure that prayer. I never took his job lightly, nor did he. Indeed, I am grateful to this fictitious character, not based upon any one individual, who helped drive me deeper into my faith and helped teach me the sublime beauty of loving others.

Would you want to write the story of a rather ordinary, sixty-something, overweight, diabetic priest in a small town?

I can't say that I honestly did. But I kept going, and didn't look back.

And look how far we have all come together. Fourteen novels. One hundred eighteen reprintings of *At Home in Mitford*. And a relationship with readers around the world who join with us to invest their own imaginations in the process of building and inhabiting a village in the mountains of North Carolina.

Over the years, I have learned to bathe my work in prayer. Say the word 'bathe.' It is a soft and caressing word. At the end of it, the tongue barely touches the upper teeth. I could dunk my work in prayer, or dip it, as into a vat, but bathing seems to work best.

It gives me true joy to open my heart to the One Who loved us first and pour out to you whatever is given. It is a very great mystery, this business of making up stories and telling them around the campfire of a book. Thanks for sitting out with me, as it were, under the stars, envisioning together the lives of so many people like you and like me, in a town that actually lives in the hearts of each of us.

Let us bathe ourselves, our family, and friends in prayer. Let us bathe our work and our enemies in prayer. And let us always come boldly to the throne of grace . . . that we may obtain mercy and find grace to help in time of need.

Selah!

And amen.

Prayer does not fit us for the greater
work. Prayer is the greater work.

—Oswald Chambers
Patches of Godlight:
Father Tim's Favorite Quotes

AT HOME IN MITFORD

In the first of fourteen Mitford novels, we meet Father Tim, an Episcopal rector yearning for more . . . until he finds himself with more than he can handle. The introduction of a dog as big as a sofa, a beautiful next-door neighbor, and the abandoned eleven-year-old Dooley shake up Father Tim's comfortable bachelor routines. He begins a new life, shedding old habits and embracing unfamiliar ones, and emerges from his cocoon along the way.

He arrived at the office, uttering the prayer he had offered at its door every morning for twelve years: 'Father, make me a blessing to someone today, through Christ our Lord. Amen.'

As he took the key from his pocket, he felt something warm and disgustingly wet on his hand.

He looked down into the face of a large, black, mud-caked dog, whose tail began to beat wildly against his pant leg.

'Good grief!' he said, wiping his hand on his windbreaker.

At that, the dog leaped up and licked his face, sending a shower of saliva into his right ear.

'Get away! Be gone!' he shouted. He tried to protect the notebook he was carrying, but the dog gave it a proper licking before he could stuff it in his jacket, then tried to snatch it from him.

'Down!' he commanded, at which the dog leaped up and gave his chin a bath.

He tried to fend the animal off with his elbow, while inserting the key in the office door. If he were a cussing man, this would offer a premier opportunity to indulge himself.

'"Let no corrupt communication proceed out of your mouth,"' he quoted in a loud voice from Ephesians, '"but that which is good to the use of edifying . . ."'

Suddenly, the dog sat down and looked at his prey with fond admiration.

—Chapter 1
Barnabas

-⁓⁓⁓-

Father Tim visits his elderly—and favorite—parishioner at the big house on the hill above Mitford.

Miss Sadie held her hands out to the rector.

'At Fernbank,' she said, 'we always hold hands when we say the blessing.'

He prayed with a contented heart. 'Accept, O Lord, our thanks and praise for all that you've done for us.* We thank you for the

---

* *The Book of Common Prayer*

blessing of family and friends, and for the loving care which surrounds us on every side. Above all, we give you thanks for the great mercies and promises given to us in Christ Jesus our Lord, in whose name we pray.'

'Amen!' they said in unison.

—Chapter 5
The Big Six-O

In this scene, Father Tim is speaking with Uncle Billy Watson, who worries that he'll lose his home. Father Tim has offered to look into a special dispensation from the town that will allow Billy and his schizophrenic wife, Miss Rose, to have life estate.

'Well, Preacher, you've took a load off my mind, and that's a fact. I've been wrestlin' with this f'r a good while, and I'm just goin' to set it down in th' road and leave it.'

'That's a good plan, Uncle Billy. God asks us not to worry about tomorrow.'

'That's a hard one, Preacher.'

'It is. And it takes practice. Just stick with today, is what he recommends. Of course, it helps to stick with him, while we're at it.'

'I've been stickin' with him a good many years. Not like I ought to, but I want t' do better, don't you know.'

'Why don't we have a prayer?' He put his arm around Uncle Billy's shoulders.

'Father, we thank you for Bill Watson's faith in you, and for his willingness to let you be in control. We turn this matter over to you now, and ask for the wisdom to proceed, through Christ, our Lord. Amen.'

—Chapter 6
Dooley

Father Tim muses on anxiety and faith.

After morning prayer, he studied the challenging message of Luke 12: 'Therefore, I tell you, do not be anxious about your life, what you shall eat, nor about your body, what you shall put on. For life is more than food, and the body more than clothing.

'Consider the ravens: they neither sow nor reap, they have neither storehouse nor barn, and yet God feeds them. Of how much more value are you than the birds?'

There was not one man in a thousand who considered these words more than poetical vapor, he thought as he dressed. Don't be anxious? Most mortals considered anxiety, and plenty of it, an absolute requirement for getting the job done. Yet, over and over again, the believer was cautioned to abandon anxiety and look only to God.

Whatever else that might be, it certainly wasn't common sense.

But 'common sense is not faith,' Oswald Chambers had written, 'and faith is not common sense.'

—Chapter 7
The One for the Job

Father Tim visits Lord's Chapel on an errand and makes a startling discovery.

As he paused to let his eyes adjust to the dimness of the Lord's Chapel nave, he heard a strange sound. Then, toward the front, on the gospel side, he saw a man kneeling in a pew. Suddenly, the man uttered such a desperate cry that the rector's heart fairly thundered.

Give me wisdom, he prayed for the second time that morning. Then he stood waiting. He didn't know for what.

'If you're up there, prove it! Show me! If you're God, you can prove it!' In the visitor's voice was a combination of anger, and odd hope.

'I'll never ask you this again,' the man said, and then, with a fury that chilled his listener, he shouted again, 'Are . . . you . . . up . . . there?'

With what appeared to be utter exhaustion, the stranger put his head in his hands as the question reverberated in the nave.

Father Tim slipped into the pew across the aisle and knelt on the cushion. 'You may be asking the wrong question.'

Startled, the man raised his head.

'I believe the question you may want to ask is "Are you down here?"'

'What kind of joke is that?'

'It isn't a joke.'

The man was neatly dressed, the rector observed, and his suit and tie appeared to be expensive. A businessman, obviously. Successful, quite likely. Not from Mitford, certainly.

'God wouldn't be God if He were only up there. In fact, another name for Him is Immanuel, which means "God with us."' He was amazed at the casual tone of his voice, as if they'd met here to chat for a while. 'He's with us right now, in this room.'

The man looked at him. 'I'd like to believe that, but I can't. I can't feel Him at all. The things I've done . . .'

'Have you asked Him to forgive the things you've done?'

'I assure you that God would not want to do that.'

'Believe it or not, I can promise that He would. In fact, He promises that He will. Would you like to ask Him into your life?'

The stranger stared into the darkened sanctuary. 'I can't do it, I've tried.'

'It isn't a test you have to pass. It doesn't require discipline and intelligence . . . not even strength and perseverance. It only requires faith.'

'I don't think I've got that.' There was a long silence. 'But I'd be willing to try . . . one more time.'

'Will you pray a simple prayer with me? On faith?'

'What do I have to lose?'

'Nothing to lose, everything to gain.' Father Tim rose from the kneeler and took the short step across the aisle, where he laid his hands on the man's head.

'If you could repeat this,' he said. 'Thank you, God, for loving me, and for sending your Son to die for my sins. I sincerely repent of my sins, and receive Christ as my personal savior. Now, as your child, I turn my entire life over to you. Amen.'

The man repeated the prayer, and they were silent.

'Is that all?' he asked the rector.

'That's all.'

'I don't know what I'm supposed to feel.'

'Whatever you feel is exactly what you're supposed to feel.'

—Chapter 11

A White Thanksgiving

A boy abandoned by his parents comes into the bachelor priest's life.

Dooley yawned and turned over. '"night,' he said.

'"night,' said the rector, putting his hand on the boy's shoulder.

Father, he prayed, silent, thank you for sending this boy into my life. Thank you for the joy and the sorrow he brings. Be with him always, to surround him with right influences, and when tests of any kind must come, give him wisdom and strength to act according to your will. Watch over his mother, also, and the other children, wherever they are. Feed and clothe them, keep them from harm, and bring them one day into a full relationship with your Son.

He sat for a long time with his hand on the sleeping boy's shoulder, feeling his heart moved with tenderness.

—Chapter 17
A Surprising Question

For months things have gone missing in the church—like a special Bible and an Orange Marmalade Cake. Father Tim and the congregation are shocked to discover that someone has been living in the attic and has been listening intently to Father Tim's sermons and prayers.

As he offered the prayer, he heard a harsh, grating noise somewhere behind him in the sanctuary. He saw the entire congregation sitting with open mouths and astonished faces, gazing toward the ceiling.

He turned around with a pounding heart, to see that the attic stairs had been let down and that someone in bare feet was descending.

He heard a single intake of breath from the congregation, a communal gasp. As the man reached the floor and stood beside the altar, he turned and gazed out at them.

He was tall and very thin, with a reddish beard and shoulder-length hair. His clothing fit loosely, as if it had been bought for someone else.

Yet, the single most remarkable thing about the incident, the rector would later say, wasn't the circumstances of the man's sudden appearance, but the unmistakable radiance on his face.

'I have a confession to make to you,' the man said to the congregation in a voice so clear, it seemed to lift the rafters. He looked at the rector, 'If you'll give me the privilege, Father.'

The man walked out in front of the communion rail and stood on the steps. 'My name,' he said, 'is George Gaynor. For the last several months, your church has been my home—and my prison. You see, I've been living behind the death bell in your attic.'

There was perfect silence in the nave.

'Until recently, this was profoundly symbolic of my life, for it was, in fact, a life of death.

'When I was a kid, I went to a church like this. An Episcopal church in Vermont where my uncle was the rector. I even thought about becoming a priest, but I learned the money was terrible. And, you see, I liked money. My father and mother liked money.

'We gave a lot of it to the church. We added a wing, we put on a shake roof, we gave the rector a Cadillac.

'It took a while to figure out what my uncle and my father were doing. My father would give thousands to the church and write it off, my uncle would keep a percentage and put the remainder in my father's Swiss bank account. Six hundred thousand dollars flowed through the alms basin into my uncle's cassock.

'When I was twelve, I began carrying on the family tradition.

'The first thing I stole was a skateboard. Later, I stole a car, and I had no regrets. My father knew everybody from the police chief to the governor. I was covered, right down the line.

'I went to the university and did pretty well. For me, getting knowledge was like getting money, getting things. It made me strong, it made me powerful. I got a Ph.D. in economics, and when I was thirty-three, I had tenure at one of the best colleges in the country.

'Then, I was in a plane crash. It was a small plane that belonged to a friend. I lay in the wreckage with the pilot, who was killed instantly, and my mother and father, who would die . . . hours later. I was pinned in the cockpit in freezing temperatures for three days, unable to move.

'Both legs were broken, my skull was fractured, the radio was demolished. Maybe you can guess what I did—I made a deal with God.

'Get me out of here, I said, and I'll clean up my act, I'll make up for what my father, my uncle, all of us, had done.

'Last summer, a friend of mine, an antique dealer, had too much to drink. He took me to his warehouse and pulled an eighteenth-century table out of the corner, and unscrewed one of its legs.

'What he pulled out of that table leg was roughly two and a half million dollars' worth of rare gems, which he'd stolen from a museum in England, in the Berkshires.

'I'd just gotten a divorce after two years of marriage, and I'd forgotten any deal I made with God in the cockpit of that Cessna.

'The bottom line is that nothing mattered to me anymore.'

George Gaynor sat down on the top step leading to the communion rail. He might have been talking to a few intimate friends in his home.

'The British authorities had gotten wind of the stuff going out of England in shipments of antiques, and my friend couldn't fence the jewels because of the FBI.

'One night, I emptied a ninety-dollar bottle of cognac into him. He told me he had hidden the jewels in one of his antique cars. I stole the keys and went to his warehouse with a hex-head wrench. I rolled under a 1937 Packard, removed the oil pan, and took the jewels home in a bag.

'I packed a few things, then I walked out on the street and stole a car. I changed the tag and started driving. I headed south.'

He stood with his hands in his pockets. 'I hadn't spoken to God in years. To tell the truth, I'd never really spoken to God but once in my life. Yet, I remembered some language from the prayer book.

'"Bless the Lord who forgiveth all our sins. His mercy endureth forever." That's what came to me as I drove. I pulled off the road and put my head down and prayed for mercy and forgiveness.

'I'd like to tell you that a great peace came over me, but I can't tell you that. There was no peace, but there was direction. I began to have a sense of where I was going, like I was attached to a fishing line, and somebody at the other end was reeling me in.

'One morning I saw an exit sign for Mitford. I took the exit, and drove straight up Main Street, and saw this church.'

His voice broke.

'I felt I'd . . . come home. I had never felt that before. I couldn't have resisted the pull God put on me, even if I tried.

'I brought my things in. Then I parked the car several blocks away and removed the tags. I walked here and started looking for a place to rest, to hide for a few days.

'That's how I came to live behind the death bell, on the platform where it's mounted. I didn't have any idea why I was in this particular place; it was as if I'd been ordered to come. But just before Thanksgiving, I found out.

'I kept my things behind the bells, but I put the jewels in an urn in your hall closet. The closet looked unused.

'During the day, I lived in the loft over the parish hall. I exercised, sat in the sun by the windows—I even learned a few hymns, to keep my mind occupied. On Sunday, I could hear every word and every note very clearly, as if we were all in the same room.

'One afternoon, I was sitting in the loft, desperate beyond anything I'd ever known. It made no sense to be here when I could be in France or South America. But I couldn't leave this place. I was powerless to leave.

'I heard the front door open, and in a few minutes, a man yelled, "Are you up there?"

'I was paralyzed with fear. This is it, I thought. Then, the call came again. But this time, I knew the question wasn't directed at me. It was directed at God.

'There was something in the voice that I recognized—the same desperation of my own soul. I told you the sound from down here carries up there, and I heard you, Father, speak to that man.

'You said the question isn't whether He's up there, but whether He's down here.'

'He told you he couldn't believe, that he felt nothing. You said it isn't a matter of feeling, it's a matter of faith. Finally, you prayed a simple prayer together.'

Remembering, the rector crossed himself. A stir ran through the congregation, a certain hum of excitement, of wonder.

'That was a real two-for-one deal, Father, because I prayed that prayer with you. You threw the line out for one, and God reeled in two.'

The congregation broke into spontaneous applause.

'After I prayed that prayer with two people I had never seen, to a God I didn't know, I came down and stole a Bible.

'As I read during the next few weeks, I began to find the most amazing peace. Even more amazing was the intimacy I was finding with God—one-on-one, moment by moment.

'I come to you this morning, urging you to discover that intimacy, if you have not.

'I also come to thank you for your hospitality, and to say to whoever made that orange cake—that was the finest cake I ever ate in my life.

'Father, thank you for calling someone to take me in.'

—Chapter 15
The Finest Sermon

❧

It was J.C. Hogan who was ringing his office phone at eight-thirty on Monday morning. 'I got a letter to the editor I need to answer,' said J.C.

'How can I help you, buddy?'

'This kid read my story about the man in the attic, about the prayer you prayed with the guy in the pew. Wrote me this letter.'

J.C. cleared his throat. '"Dear Editor, What exactly was the prayer the preacher prayed when the man in the attic got saved? My daddy wants to know and I do too. Thank you."'

'Do you want me to write it down and drop it by, or just tell you on the phone?'

'Phone's fine,' said J.C., breathing heavily into the receiver.

'Thank you, God, for loving me, and for sending your Son to die for my sins . . .'

'Got it,' said J.C.

'I repent of my sins and receive Jesus Christ as my personal savior.'

'Got it.'

'And now, as your child . . .'

'As your what?'

'As your child.'

'Got it.'

'I turn my entire life over to you. Amen.'

'What's the big deal with this prayer? It looks like some little Sunday school thing to me. It's too simple.'

'It's the very soul of simplicity. Yet it can transform a life completely when prayed with the right spirit.'

—Chapter 18

Something to Think About

Miss Sadie, a longtime benefactor of Lord's Chapel, has just finished telling Father Tim her tragic love story.

Father Tim got up from his chair and placed a hand on her fragile shoulder. 'Father,' he prayed, 'I ask you to heal any vestige of bitter hurt in your child, Sadie, and by the power of your Holy Spirit, bring to her mind and heart, now and forever, only those memories which serve to restore, refresh, and delight. Through Jesus Christ, your Son our Lord, Amen.'

'Amen!' she said, reaching up to put her hand on his.

—Chapter 19
A Love Story

Dooley and Father Tim pray for Dooley's missing siblings, who Dooley helped raise when his mother couldn't care for them.

'Do you know where they are?' he asked Dooley.

'Mama said she'd never tell nobody, or th' state would come git 'em. I was th' last'n t' go.'

If it wrenched his heart to hear this, how must Dooley's heart be faring? 'Have you ever prayed for your brothers and your baby sister?'

'Nope.'

'Prayer is a way to stay close to them. You can't see them, but you can pray for them, and God will hear that prayer. It's the best thing you can do for them right now.'

'How d'you do it?'

'You just jump in and do it. Something like this. You can say it with me. Our Father . . .'

'Our Father . . .'

'Be with my brother Kenny and help him . . .'

'Be 'ith m' brother, Kenny, an' he'p him . . .'

'To be strong, to be brave, to love you and love me . . .'

'T' be strong, t' be brave, t' love you an' love me . . .'

'No matter what the circumstances . . .'

'No matter what th' circumstances.'

'And please, God . . .'

'An' please, God . . .'

'Be with those whose names Dooley will bring you right now . . .'

He heard something hard and determined in the boy's voice. 'Mama. Granpaw. Jessie an' Sammy an' Poobaw. Miz Ivey at church, an' Tommy . . . 'at ol' dog, Barnabas . . . m' rabbit . . . Miz Coppersmith an' ol' Vi'let an' all.'

—Chapter 20
Baxter Park

Father Tim's neighbor, Cynthia Coppersmith, has his head spinning—to say the least.

Lord, he prayed, I'm not used to this dating business. Some might tell me to follow my instincts, but I've spent so many years trying to follow yours that I've nearly lost the hang of following mine. So, thank you for being in on this and handling it to please yourself.

—Chapter 21
The Bells

Recently diagnosed with diabetes, Tim is in a coma after eating more than enough of the legendary Orange Marmalade Cake.

He was not surprised to see that the Spurgeons were having fish for dinner. But he was surprised to see the Lord sitting at the table in the high-ceilinged room. He felt his heart hammer in his throat.

'Timothy, I have a purpose for this time in your life.'

'Yes, Lord.' The hammering ceased, a sweet peace invaded him; he was floating.

He ascended through the roof of the rectory and over the village, above the monument that anchored the little town, and Lew Boyd's Esso, where Coot and Lew were looking up and waving to him as he passed.

He found that he had great wings, the wings of a butterfly. They were iridescent yellow and purple, and buoyed him along without effort. Indeed, the movement of his wings wasn't for the sake of keeping him aloft, but was for joy's sake alone.

The people were dressed in white and led in procession by a young priest bearing a wooden cross.

He placed the cross in a newly dug hole near the church door, and dirt was cast into the hole, and the children brought flowers and pressed their roots into the damp earth.

Then the priest lifted his hands and prayed, thanking God for new life and for hope. 'As He left the shroud of death and rose to new life, so this butterfly, once trapped in a cocoon, has become free. Go in new life with Christ. Go, and be as the butterfly.'

The butterfly lifted its wings and soared over the church. There was a cool, sudden breeze, the kind found in the brewing of a storm that moves in from the west.

The butterfly passed over the town anchored by the monument; over Fernbank on the hill in the orchards. Then there was the slate roof of the rectory, and the red roof of the yellow house next door.

His head felt thick, as if he had been drugged, or struck a blow. Uneasily, he rolled over and saw someone sitting in the glow of his bedside lamp.

Cynthia put her hand on his forehead. He could not speak, nor could he understand her when she spoke. 'Timothy,' she said. 'I'm here.'

—Chapter 23

Homecoming

Weeks later, Father Tim prepares to go to England—a trip given to him by his parishioners.

He was dreading it, dreading it all. He had not been in an airplane in nine years, and to fly across the ocean was suddenly unthinkable. Travel always sounded wonderful when one considered the end, but to consider the means was quite another story.

He sat in his chair in the bedroom and looked at the results of his feeble packing effort. He wouldn't leave for four days yet, but he thought it best to start working on that aggravating project.

'Timothy,' he said aloud, causing Barnabas to look around, 'you have a rotten attitude about this trip. Back up and start over! Thank you, Lord, for the opportunity to go to this wonderful part of your world, thank you for making provision through the sacrifices of so many people, and for bringing it all together in a way that is clear evidence of your grace.

'Thank you for the good home for Dooley and Barnabas. Forgive me for being dark-spirited about what is certainly a privilege. Enable me to take care of every need before I go. And, Lord, show me what to pack.'

He felt as if he were emerging from a long, narrow hallway, from a cocoon, perhaps. He felt a weight lifting off his shoulders as the commuter plane lifted its wings over the fields.

Go in new life with Christ, he said to himself, wondering at the strangely familiar thought.

Go, and be as the butterfly.

—Chapter 24
In New Life

Worry about nothing. Pray about everything.

—Wayside pulpit
(Father Tim calls this shorthand for Philippians 4:6)

A LIGHT IN THE WINDOW

In the second Mitford novel, Father Tim's love affair with Cynthia takes center stage. Can he fit his newfound love into his habit-filled life? And Dooley into their future as a family?

Attending a town council meeting was decidedly not what he wanted to do with his evening. But he would go; it might put him back in the swing of things, and frankly, he was curious why the mayor, Esther Cunningham, had called an unofficial meeting and why it might concern him.

'Don't eat,' Esther told him on the phone. 'Ray's bringin' baked beans, cole slaw, and ribs from home. Been cookin' all day.'

There was a quickening in the air of the mayor's office. Ray was setting out his home-cooked supper on the vast desktop.

'Mayor,' said Leonard Bostick, 'it's a cryin' shame you cain't cook as good as Ray.'

'I've got better things to do,' she snapped. 'I did the cookin' for forty years. Now it's his turn.'

Ray grinned. 'You tell 'em, honey.'

'Whooee!' said Paul Hartley. 'Baby backs! Get over here, Father, and give us a blessin'.'

'Come on!' shouted the mayor to the group lingering in the hall. 'It's blessin' time!'

Esther Cunningham held out her hands, and the group eagerly formed a circle.

'Our Lord,' said the rector, 'we're grateful for the gift of friends and neighbors and those willing to lend their hand to the welfare of this place. We thank you for the peace of our village and for your grace to do the work that lies ahead. We thank you, too, for this food and ask a special blessing on the one who prepared it. In Jesus' name.'

'Amen!' said the assembly.

—Chapter 1
Close Encounters

Cynthia has been in Manhattan for much of a brutal winter, and her flight home today will surely be canceled. Is there no balm in Gilead?

He held out hope until the morning Cynthia was to arrive. It had rained the day before, and now, at dawn, he heard the relentless freezing rain still rapping sharply against the windows. Flights would be canceled, airports shut down.

He prayed they would be able to go forward with the hanging of the greens and with the afternoon and midnight services on Christmas Eve. After the death of winter had lain upon them like a pall, they needed the breathing life of the Child; they were starving for it.

He continued to pray for Miss Rose and Uncle Billy, Miss Sadie and Louella, and for all who were elderly, sick, or without food or heat. He was bold to ask that angels be sent, and step on it.

—Chapter 6
Water Like a Stone

Yesterday, he and Dooley had bumped elbows in the kitchen, splashing soda from their glasses onto the floor. As they squatted down to wipe it up, the dark liquid of Dooley's Coke ran into the colorless liquid of his Diet Sprite. You couldn't tell where one began and the other left off. Was he willing to blend into the life of another human being for the rest of his days, and have Cynthia blend into his?

That, of course, was Scripture's bottom line on marriage: one flesh. Not two autonomous beings merely coming together at dinnertime or brushing past one another in the hallway, holding on to their singleness.

If he could do the thing at all, could he stick it through? Would he be of one mind at the church altar and of another mind later? Could he trust himself?

The essay he read yesterday had called the power to love truly and devotedly 'a sacred fire, not to be burned before idols.'

A sacred fire. And if sacred, then durable? The word held a mild comfort. A durable fire.

Lord, take this fear and dash it. Rebuke the enemy who is the creator of all fear, and give me grace to be the man you've called me to be, no matter what lies in store. If I'm to spend the rest of my life with her, then open the door wide. Swing it open, I pray! And if this is not pleasing to you, well, then . . .

He could not imagine the other, could not imagine going on without her. Even in prayer, his heart was fickle and deceitful, turning this way and that.

—Chapter 10
Cousins

'We are not necessarily doubting,' said C. S. Lewis, 'that God will do the best for us; we are wondering how painful the best will turn out to be.'

He had spent an hour on his knees, asking for the best, believing in the best, thanking God in advance for the best. No, he didn't doubt that God would do the best for Cynthia and for him. But yes, he was wondering how painful the best might be.

—Chapter 12
Faith Not Feeling

Dearest Cynthia,

Your bright spirit is the light of my life. When I read the gracious things you would do to make me happy, my foolish limitations and fogyisms are humiliating to me.

Your openness has widened the door of my heart, somehow, and I feel a tenderness for you that is nearly overwhelming. I can't think how I could be worth the care you take with me, the effort you expend, and the ceaseless patience you bring to our friendship.

For this alone, I must love you.

My dearest,

You would be amused if you knew how long I have sat and looked at the two words just above, words that I have never written to anyone in my life. Can it have taken more than six decades for these words to form in my spirit, and then, without warning, to appear on the paper before me, with such naturalness and ease?

Even for this alone, I love you.

I've come across a letter from Robert Browning to EBB, in which he says:

'I would not exchange the sadness of being away from you for any imaginable delight in which you had no part.'

To this sentiment, I say Selah!

I also say good night, my dearest love. You are ever in my prayers.

Timothy

—Chapter 13
More Than Music

Do not look forward to what may happen tomorrow; the same everlasting Father will take care of you tomorrow and every day. Either He will shield you from suffering, or He will give you unfailing strength to bear it. Be at peace, put aside all anxious thoughts and imaginations, and say continually: 'The Lord is my strength and my shield; my heart has trusted in Him and I am helped. He is not only with me . . . but in me . . . and I in Him.'

—St. Francis de Sales
A Continual Feast: Words of Comfort and Celebration,
Collected by Father Tim

THESE HIGH, GREEN HILLS

At last, Father Tim has married his thoughtful and vivacious neighbor, Cynthia. This novel follows the couple as they begin their common life, navigating struggles great and small—like getting lost in a cave on a life-changing camping trip. Meanwhile, Sadie Baxter celebrates a big birthday—'in the nick of time,' as someone would later say—and a total stranger to Father Tim becomes a key player in the series.

At Lord's Chapel, the arrangements on the altar became gourds and pumpkins, accented by branches of the fiery red maple. At this time of year, the rector himself liked doing the floral offerings. He admitted it was a favorite season, and his preaching, someone remarked, grew as electrified as the sharp, clean air.

'Take them,' he said on Sunday morning, lifting the cup and the Host toward the people, 'in remembrance that Christ died for you, and feed on Him in your hearts by faith, with thanksgiving.'

Giving his own wife the Host was an act that might never cease to move and amaze him. More than sixty years a bachelor, and now this—seeing her face look up expectantly, and feeling the warmth of her hand as he placed the bread in her palm. 'The body of our Lord Jesus Christ, which was given for you, Cynthia.'*

He couldn't help but see the patch of colored light that fell on her hair through the stained-glass window by the rail, as if she were being appointed to something divine. Surely there could be no divinity in having to live the rest of her life with him, with his set-in-concrete ways and infernal diabetes.

They walked home together after church, hand in hand, his sermon notebook tucked under his arm. He felt as free as a schoolboy, as light as air. How could he ever have earned God's love, and hers into the bargain?

The point was, he couldn't. It was all grace, and grace alone.

—Chapter 1
Through the Hedge

Singing in bed! That's a nice thought.

'Save us from troubled, restless sleep,' he sang in the darkened room, 'from all ill dreams Your children keep . . .'

'How lovely,' she murmured, lying beside him. 'What are you singing?'

'A verse from Louella's hymn, "To You before the close of day . . . "'

He sang again, '. . . so calm our minds that fears may cease, and rested bodies wake in peace.'

---

* *The Book of Common Prayer*, Holy Eucharist I

'Amen,' she whispered, taking his hand.

—Chapter 3
Gathered In

This may well be my favorite exhortation of St. Paul.

He despised losing sleep over any issue. Broad daylight was the time for fretting and wrestling—if it had to be done. 'Don't worry about anything,' Paul had written to the church at Philippi, 'but in everything, by prayer and supplication, make your requests known unto God. And the peace that passes all understanding will fill your hearts and minds through Christ Jesus.' In the last hour, he had twice given his worries to God and then snatched them back, only to lie here, anxious, staring at the ceiling.

—Chapter 4
Passing the Torch

Father Tim meets—for the first time—the 'key player' we mentioned earlier.

He walked up to Fernbank after he left the office, to check on Miss Sadie's house.

He was halfway up the bank and had stopped to rest when he saw movement ahead, among the ferns. It looked like a young boy, who was facing away from him.

He watched intently. The boy was digging ferns with their root balls, and putting them into a sack, looking to the left and right, but not behind.

Certain people, he recalled, often dug ferns and rhododendron on someone else's property and sold them to nurseries who looked the other way. He knew, too, about the flourishing traffic in galax leaves, and local moss, that was peeled off the ground and pulled from logs in unbroken sheets and sold to florists.

The ways and means of making a living in these mountains had never been easy, he knew that, but let an incident like this go by, and Fernbank could be stripped of the very resource that inspired its name.

The boy took off his hat. Long hair spilled down and fell over his shoulders. Actually, it appeared to be a girl, a girl wearing boy's clothes, or even a man's clothes, given the way they hung on her. She had sashed the oversized shirt with vines.

'Hello,' he called.

She whirled around, letting the mattock drop. He saw the fear in her eyes, then the anger.

'I ain't done nothin',' she said harshly, standing her ground as he walked toward her. He saw that she noted his clerical collar.

The point was to speak kindly, he thought. She might have been a wild rabbit for the look in her eyes and the fierce way she glared at him. He knew a thing or two about rabbits, having raised them as a boy. They didn't like sudden moves.

'These ferns are pretty special.'

'I don't care nothin' about 'em.'

She backed away from him and put her foot on the mattock handle.

He stopped about a yard from her and glanced toward the sack.

'I'll knock you in th' head if you lay hands on my sack. I don't care if you are a preacher.'

'Miss Sadie Baxter's ferns are a town treasure.' He spoke as if he had all the time in the world. If he had a stick, he would have whittled it with his pocket knife. 'These banks have been covered with the wild cinnamon fern for many years—there's not another stand like it anywhere.'

'Don't mean nothin' t' me,' she said, edging toward the sack.

'Ferns grow in families, like most other kinds of plants. Actually, there are four different fern families . . . and look at this. See how the leaves curl at the tip of the stem? That's called a fiddlehead.'

She was going to grab the mattock and sack and run for it; he could tell by the language of her movements.

'I'd personally appreciate it if you'd replant everything you just dug,' he said. 'In fact, I'll even help you do it. And I won't say anything to anybody about it, unless I see you here again.'

She reached down and grabbed the mattock and dived toward the sack. Quick as lightning, she threw it over her shoulder and was away, racing down the bank like a hare.

He saw she was barefoot and that she'd left her hat lying at his feet.

Had he done or said the right thing? He didn't know. He had never liked the pressure to do and say the right thing because he was a preacher. He was also a human being, and he stumbled along like the rest of humankind.

He squinted his eyes and watched her disappear over the curve of the green bank.

She had not looked back.

—Chapter 8
Serious About Fun

-ᢌᢌ᠊᠂᠊ᢢ᠊ᢢᢢ-

'How lucky you are!' people continually said to him. But, no. There was never any time he thought of it as luck. Luck! What was that, after all, but so much random good fortune? It was grace, and grace alone that brought Cynthia's body close to his, made them this single mystical flesh that, once laced together like brandy in coffee, could not be riven apart—even by the world and its unending pressures.

He closed his eyes and thanked God for the crucible of peace and laughter and love that lay beside him, snoring with galvanized precision.

—Chapter 9
Locked Gates

-ᢌᢌ᠊᠂᠊ᢢ᠊ᢢᢢ-

So they go on a camping trip with the church youth group and get lost in a cave. Did you know you can get lost in a cave in less than five minutes? Scary. But for Father Tim, good. Very good. By the way, I dropped (literally) into a wild cave to research this episode. Never again.

Her voice seemed to come from somewhere above him. He reached up, feeling nothing but air, then touched a flat rock. He inched his hand along the edge, and found the tip of her tennis shoe. 'You're standing on some kind of ledge. Back up a little, and take it easy.'

'Timothy . . .'

'Don't panic. I'm fine. We've got to be near the entrance. We'll be out of here in no time. Stay calm.'

'Let me give you a hand.'

'Back up and stay put.'

He grabbed the ledge and hauled himself up. He had fallen only a couple of feet, thanks be to God.

Lord, You know I'm completely in the dark, in more ways than one. I don't have a clue where we are or what to do. I know You're there, I know You'll answer, give me some supernatural understanding here. . . .

He stood up and leaned against the wall, and reached for her, and found her sleeve and took her hand. He had lost all sense of time. *A thousand years in Thy sight are but as yesterday when it is past, and as a watch in the night. . . .* Was he being introduced to something like God's own sense of time?

—Chapter 10
The Cave

Why hadn't they left a sign at the entrance of the cave, like their nearly empty water bottle or a candy wrapper? It might have said, *If you find this, we're still in here. Start the search.*

Stay calm was still the directive. They couldn't go blasting down every passageway that presented itself. Light! If only he had the tiniest flame, the barest flicker of illumination, he would fall to his knees in thanksgiving.

In Him was life; and the life was the light of men. And the light shineth in the darkness; and the darkness overcame it not. . . .

He refused to fear this thick, palpable darkness. As far as he knew, God had not drawn the line on caves. He hadn't said, *I'll stick by you as long as you don't do some fool thing like get lost in a cave.* What He had said was, *I will never leave you. Period.*

'Trust God!' he blurted to his wife.

—Chapter 10
The Cave

Miss Sadie was wearing a blue dress with a lace collar and one of her mother's hand-painted brooches. He didn't think he'd ever seen her looking finer. Her wrist appeared almost normal, and the car key was hanging on a hook in the kitchen, untouched in recent months.

They sat down to green beans and cornbread, with glasses of cold milk all around, and held hands as he asked the blessing.

'Lord, we thank You for the richness of this life and our friendship, and for this hot, golden-crusted cornbread. Please bless the hands that prepared it, and make us ever mindful of the needs of others. Amen!'

'. . . You didn't say nothin' to th' Lord 'bout my beans,' said Louella.

He had received nothing in that hour at church but a sense of calm. That in itself was an answer, but not the one he was looking for.

Forgiveness.

He felt the word slowly inscribe itself on his heart, and knew at once. This was the answer.

'Forgiveness,' he said aloud. 'Forgiveness is the lesson of the cave. . . .'

He sat still, and waited.

'And what about Dooley, Lord? Why does Dooley pull away from us?'

Again, a kind of inscription.

Ditto.

He shook his head. Ditto? God didn't talk like that; God didn't say ditto. He laughed out loud. Ditto?

He felt his spirit lifting.

Ditto! Of course God talks like that, if He wants to.

—Chapter 13
Homecoming

'Happy Birthday, Miss Sadie!' The children held up posters they had made for the occasion.

The entire room burst into hoots, cheers, and applause as he offered his arm and led the guest of honor to a chair in front of the fireplace.

'I'd better sit down before I fall down!' she warbled.

Laughter all around.

'Please come and pay your respects to our precious friend on the morning of her ninetieth birthday,' said the rector. 'Help yourself to the refreshments, and save room for cake and ice cream after the mayor's speech. But first, let's pray!'

Much shuffling around and grabbing of loose toddlers.

'Our Father, we thank You profoundly for this day, that we might gather to celebrate ninety years of a life well-lived, of time well-spent in your service.

'We thank You for the roof on this house which was given by Your child, Sadie Baxter, and for all the gifts she freely shares from what You graciously provide.

'We thank You for her good health, her strong spirits, her bright hope, and her laughter. We thank You for Louella, who brings the zestful seasoning of love into our lives. And we thank You, Lord, for the food You've bestowed on this celebration, and regard with thanksgiving how blessed we are in all things. Continue to go with Sadie, we pray, and keep her as the apple of Your eye. We ask this in Jesus' name.'

—Chapter 15
And Many More

A female burn patient, identified only as LM, has been checked into Mitford Hospital.

As he opened the door to the gray room, he felt he was stepping into a place removed, out of time.

He walked to the bed and looked at what he could see of the patient. Only a small portion of the right side of her face was visible, distorted by the large tube that entered her mouth. The smell of saline, which permeated the dressings, came to him like a sour wind from the sea. Dear God. Could he speak?

The patient opened her eye and gazed into his, and he suddenly felt a surge of power to do this thing.

'You're not alone. I'm with you. I've asked the Holy Spirit to be with us, also.'

He had seen eyes that beseeched him from the very soul, but he hadn't seen anything like this.

The thought seemed to come from a place in him as deep as the patient's desperation. 'I'm asking God to give me some of your pain,' he said, hoarse with feeling. 'I'll share it with you.'

She looked at him again and closed her eye.

He moved the chair next to her bed, and sat down.

Lord, give me grace to do what I just said I'd do. Whatever it takes.

—Chapter 17
Sing On!

Just down the hall from LM, Miss Sadie is suffering from a serious fall—the sort of thing that can send an embolism on a fatal journey to the heart.

'I'm going in to talk with LM a few minutes,' said the rector, 'then I'll step down the hall to Miss Sadie. How is she?'

Hoppy ran his fingers through his graying hair. He started to speak, then changed his mind.

He stood by LM's bed and held the rail and watched the random flickering of the lid over her closed eye. The air in the tube that formed her breath sounded harsh against the constant hiss and gurgle of the IV drips.

He prayed aloud, but kept his voice quiet. 'Our Father, thank You for being with us, for we can't bear this alone. Cool and soothe, heal and restore, love and protect. Comfort and unite those concerned for her, and keep them in Your care. We're asking for Your best here, Lord, we're expecting it.'

She opened her eye and he looked into the deep well of it, feeling a strangely familiar connection.

'Hey, there,' he said.

—Chapter 17
Sing On!

⚬⟶⚬

After tolling the death bell, the rector went to Lilac Road and sat with Louella and prayed the ancient prayer of commendation: 'Acknowledge, we humbly beseech You, a sheep of Your own fold, a lamb of Your own flock. . . . Receive Sadie Eleanor Baxter into the arms of Your mercy, into the blessed rest of everlasting peace, and into the glorious company of the saints. . . .'*

Then he did what others after him would do with Sadie Baxter's lifelong friend. He sat and wept with her, sobbing like a child.

—Chapter 18
Every Trembling Heart

⚬⟶⚬

'The people have gathered, the trumpets have sounded!' he exclaimed. 'Sadie Eleanor Baxter is at home and at peace, and I charge us all to be filled with the joy of this wondrous fact.'

How often had people heard that, for a Christian, death is but the ultimate triumph, a thing to celebrate? The hope was that it cease being a fact believed with the head, and become a truth known by the heart, as he now knew it.

He looked out to the congregation who packed the nave, and saw that they knew it too. They had caught the spark. A kind of warming fire ran through the place, kindled with excitement and wonder.

When Louella sang, her voice mingled powerfully with Dooley's. She had a big contralto voice. Their music flooded the church with a high consolation.

---

* *The Book of Common Prayer*

Jesus, Thou art all compassion
Pure, unbounded love Thou art
Visit us with Thy salvation
Enter every trembling heart . . .

Into the silence that followed the music, and true to his Baptist roots, Absalom Greer raised a heartfelt 'Amen!'

The rector looked to the pew where Sadie Baxter had sat for the fifteen years he had been in this pulpit, and saw Olivia and Hoppy, Louella and Absalom holding hands. Those left behind. . . .

'We don't know,' he said, in closing, 'who among us will be the next to go, whether the oldest or the youngest. We pray that he or she will be gently embraced by death, have a peaceful end, and a glorious resurrection in Christ.

'But for now, let us go in peace—to love and serve the Lord.'

'Thanks be to God!' said the congregation, meaning it.

The trumpets blew mightily, and the people moved to the church lawn, where Esther Bolick's three-tiered cake sat on a fancy table, where the ECW had stationed jars of lemonade, and where, as any passerby could see, a grand celebration was under way.

—Chapter 18
Every Trembling Heart

Dear God, be good to me, the sea is so wide and my boat is so small.

—Prayer of Breton fisherman

OUT TO CANAAN

In *Out to Canaan*, Father Tim and Cynthia ponder retirement. We get to know Lace Turner, and watch as Dooley continues to find his way. Meanwhile, Mack Stroupe is running for mayor, with plans to build a luxury spa in Mitford, and Buck Leeper takes a detour on his journey to self-destruction.

Thanks be to God, Lace was now in the care of the Harpers and doing surprisingly well at Mitford School. Naturally, she continued to use her native dialect, but she had dazzled them all with her reading skills and quick intelligence. He was even more taken, however, by the extraordinary depth of her character.

Another Dooley Barlowe, in a sense—with all of Dooley's thorny spirit, and then some.

He opened the screen door and called. Olivia rushed down the hall and gave him a hug.

'Father, you're always there for us.'

'And you for us,' he said.

'She's in her room, packing. I'm sorry to be so . . . so inept. . . .'

'You're not inept. You're trying to raise a teenager and deal with a broken spirit.' He looked into her violet eyes, which he always found remarkable, and saw her frantic concern. He had been there with Dooley and would go there again.

He took Olivia's hands. 'Father, this is serious business. Give us your wisdom, we pray, to do what is just, what is healing, what is needed. Give us discernment, also, by the power of your Holy Spirit, and soften our hearts toward one another and toward you. In Jesus' name.'

'Amen!' she said, weeping.

—Chapter 3
Eden

Amazing grace; Father Tim learns that LM is Pauline Barlowe, Dooley's mother.

He saw the light in Pauline's face, the softness of expression as she looked upon her scrubbed and freckled children. Thanks be to God! Three out of five. . . .

He sat down, feeling expansive, and waited until all hands were clasped, linking them together in a circle.

'Our God and our Father, we thank You!' he began.

'Thank You, Jesus!' boomed Louella in happy accord.

'We thank You with full hearts for this family gathered here tonight, and ask Your mercy and blessings upon all those who hunger, not only for sustenance, but for the joy, the peace, and the one true salvation which You, through Your Son, freely offer. . . .'

—Chapter 11
Amazing Grace

⸻

I love this scene and hope you will, too.

The rector might have come to the church alone and given thanks on his knees in the empty nave. But he'd delighted in inviting one and all to a service that would express his own private thanksgiving.

He came briskly down the aisle in his robe, and turned.

'*Grace to you and peace from God our Father and from the Lord Jesus Christ!*' he quoted from Philippians.

'*I will bless the Lord who gives me counsel,*' he said with the psalmist, '*my heart teaches me, night after night. I have set the Lord always before me; because He is at my right hand, I shall not fall.*'

He spoke the ancient words of the sheep farmer, Amos: '*Seek Him who made the Pleiades and Orion, and turns deep darkness into the morning, and darkens the day into night; who calls for the waters of the sea and pours them out upon the surface of the earth: the Lord is His name!*'

There it was, the smile he was seeking from his wife. And lo, not one but two, because Dooley was giving him a grin into the bargain.

'Dear friends in Christ, here in the presence of Almighty God, let us kneel in silence, and with patient and obedient hearts confess our sins, so that we may obtain forgiveness by His infinite goodness and mercy.'

Here it comes, thought Adele Hogan, who, astonishing herself, slid off the worn oak pew onto the kneeler.

Hope Winchester couldn't do it; she was as frozen as a mullet, and felt her heart pounding like she'd drunk a gallon of coffee. Maybe she'd leave, who would notice anyway, with their heads bowed, but the thing was, there was always somebody who probably wasn't keeping his eyes closed, and would see her dart away like a convict. . . .

'Most merciful God,' Esther Bolick prayed aloud and in unison with the others from the Book of Common Prayer, 'we confess that we have sinned against You in thought, word, and deed . . .'

She felt the words enter her aching bones like balm.

'. . . by what we have done,' prayed Gene, 'and by what we have left undone.'

'We have not loved You with our whole heart,' intoned Uncle Billy Watson, squinting through a magnifying glass to see the words in the prayer book, 'we have not loved our neighbors as ourselves.'

He found the words of the prayer beautiful. They made him feel hopeful and closer to the Lord, and maybe it was true that he hadn't always done right by his neighbors, but he would try to do better, he would start before he hit the street this very night. He quickly offered a silent thanks that somebody would be driving them home afterward, since it was pitch-dark out there, and still hot as a depot stove into the bargain.

'We are truly sorry and we humbly repent,' prayed Pauline Barlowe, unable to keep the tears back.

'For the sake of Your Son Jesus Christ, have mercy on us and forgive us,' prayed Cynthia Kavanagh, amazed all over again at how she'd come to be kneeling in this place, and hoping that the stress she'd recently seen in her husband was past, and that this service would mark the beginning of renewal and refreshment.

'. . . that we may delight in Your will, and walk in Your ways,' prayed Sophia Burton, wishing with all her heart that she could do that very thing every day of her life, really do it and not just pray it—but then, maybe she could, she was beginning to feel like she could . . . maybe.

'. . . to the glory of Your Name!'* prayed the rector, feeling his spirit moved toward all who were gathered in this place.

—Chapter 15
Day into Night

Buck Leeper is one of my favorite characters. During work on this book, I occasionally found myself praying for him. He made a U-turn in a fast-food parking lot and came back to Mitford to find what we all hunger for.

Father Tim looked at the man who had controlled some of the biggest construction jobs in the Southeast, but couldn't, at this moment, control the shaking.

'I pulled into an Arby's parkin' lot and sat in the car and tried to pray,' said Buck. 'The only thing that came was somethin' I'd heard all those years in my grandaddy's church. I said, Thy will be done.'

'That's the prayer that never fails.'

The clock ticked. Buck gazed into the fire.

---

* Full prayer from *The Book of Common Prayer*

'He can be for your life what the foundation is for a building.'

'I want to do whatever it takes, Father.'

'It can take only a simple prayer. Some think it's too simple, but if you pray it with your heart, it can change everything. Will you pray it with me?'

'What will happen when I do it?'

'You mean what will happen now, tonight, in this room?'

'Yes.'

'Something extraordinary could happen. Or it could be so subtle, so gradual, you'll never know the exact moment He comes in.'

The rector held out his hand to a man he'd come to love, and they stood before the fire and bowed their heads.

'Thank you, God, for loving me . . .'

'Thank You, God . . .' Buck hesitated and went on, 'for loving me.'

'. . . and for sending Your Son to die for my sins. I sincerely repent of my sins, and receive Christ as my personal savior.'

The superintendent repeated the words slowly, carefully.

'Now, as Your child, I turn my entire life over to You.'

'. . . as Your child,' said Buck, weeping quietly, 'I turn my entire life over to You.'

'Amen.'

'Amen.'

—Chapter 21
Lion and Lamb

Pray as you can, and do not try to pray as you can't.

—John Chapman, English Benedictine monk

A NEW SONG

Father Tim has retired, and agrees to serve as interim priest of St. John's in the Grove on Whitecap Island. He and Cynthia encounter serious challenges, as big trouble brews back home. What was Dooley *thinking?* And who would steal the valuable statue from his mantel in Mitford?

Before he and Cynthia depart for the Outer Banks area, he pauses to meditate on what may lie ahead.

He loved Cynthia Kavanagh; she'd become the very life of his heart, and no, he would never turn back from her laughter and tears and winsome ways. But tonight, looking at the chimneys against the glow of the streetlight, he mourned that time of utter freedom, when nobody expected him home or cared whether he arrived, when he could sit with a book in his lap, snoring in the wing chair, a fire turning to embers on the hearth. . . .

He raised his hand to the rectory in a type of salute, and closed his eyes as the bells of Lord's Chapel began their last peal of the day.

Bong . . .

'Lord,' he said aloud, 'Your will be done in our lives.'

Bong . . .

'Guard me from self-righteousness, and from any looking to myself in this journey.'

Bong . . .

'I believe Whitecap is where You want us, and we know that You have riches for us there.'

Bong . . .

'Prepare our hearts for this parish, and theirs to receive us.'

Bong . . .

'Thank You for the blessing of Cynthia and Dooley; for this place and this time, and yes, Lord, even for this change. . . .'

Bong . . .

Bong . . .

The bells pealed twice before he acknowledged and named the fear in his heart.

'Forgive this fear in me which I haven't confessed to You until now.'

Bong . . .

'You tell us that You do not give us the spirit of fear, but of power, and of love, and of a sound mind.'

Bong . . .

'Gracious God . . .' He paused.

'I surrender myself to You completely . . . again.'

He took a deep breath and held it, then let it out slowly, and realized he felt the peace, the peace that didn't always come, but came now.

—Chapter 3
Going, Going, Gone

He and Cynthia arrive in Whitecap during a storm, spend a miserable night in the wrong house, and are finally given safe harbor by new friends and parishioners.

He'd faced it time and again in his years as a priest—how do you pour out a heart full of thanksgiving in a way that even dimly expresses your joy?

He reached for the hands of the Fieldwalkers.

'Father, You're so good. So good to bring us out of the storm into the light of this new day, and into the company of these new friends.

'Touch, Lord, the hands and heart and spirit of Marion, who prepared this food for us when she might have done something more important.

'Bless this good man for looking out for us, and waiting up for us, and gathering the workers who labored to make this a bright and shining home.

'Lord, we could be here all morning only thanking You, but we intend to press forward and enjoy the pleasures of this glorious feast which You have, by Your grace, put before us. We thank You again for Your goodness and mercy, and for tending to the needs of those less fortunate, through Christ our Lord. Amen.'

'Amen!'

—Chapter 5
A Patch of Blue

Father Tim stood at the foot of the steps inhaling the new smells of his new church, set like a gem into the heart of his new parish. St. John's winsome charm made him feel completely at home, expectant as a child.

He crossed himself and prayed aloud, spontaneous.

'Thank You, Lord! What a blessing . . . and what a challenge. Give me patience, Father, for what may come, and especially I ask for Your healing grace in the body of St. John's.'

—Chapter 5
A Patch of Blue

He sat in the church office, hearing rain peck the windowpanes like chickens after corn, and read from a sermon of Charles Spurgeon, delivered at Newington on March 9, 1873.

I tell thee what I would have thee do . . .

Go to Him without fear or trembling; ere yon sun goes down and ends this day of mercy, go and tell Him thou hast broken the Father's laws—tell Him that thou art lost, and thou needest to be saved; appeal to His manly heart, and to His brotherly sympathies.

Pour out thy broken heart at His feet: let thy soul flow over
in His presence, and I tell thee He cannot cast thee away . . .

He jotted in his sermon notebook: *Not that He <u>will</u> not turn a deaf*
ear, but that He <u>cannot</u>. Press this truth. Spurgeon had put into a nut-
shell what he wanted to preach on Sunday to the body at St. John's.

. . . though thy prayer be feeble as the spark in the flax, He will
not quench it; and though thy heart be bruised like a reed, He
will not break it.
    May the Holy Spirit bless you with a desire to go to God
through Jesus Christ; and encourage you to do so by showing that
He is meek and lowly of heart, gentle, and tender, full of pity.

Bottom line, he would tell his congregation what Nike had told
the world:
    Just do it.

—Chapter 8
The Spark in the Flax

- ·⊰⊱ ❧ ⊰⊱· -

Glorious! His congregation was standing bolt upright, and singing as
lustily as any crowd of Baptists.

    'Lift high the cross
    the love of Christ proclaim . . .'

With his flock, he gave himself wholly to the utterance of joy on
this morning of mornings.

'. . . till all the world adore
his sacred Name.
Led on their way by
this triumphant sign
the hosts of God in
conquering ranks combine.'

The organ music flooded the nave like a great incoming tide; surely he only imagined seeing the chandeliers tremble.

He lifted his hands and prayed.

'Almighty God, to You all hearts are open, all desires known, and from You no secrets are hid: Cleanse the thoughts of our hearts by the inspiration of Your Holy Spirit, that we may perfectly love You, and worthily magnify Your holy Name; through Christ our Lord.'*

'Amen!' they said as one.

—Chapter 10
If Wishes Were Horses

Cynthia has given her husband the gift of a deep-sea fishing experience. He goes, of course, but I can assure you that he will not do this again. We print almost all of the chapter because, for good reason, it is a very prayer-full tale.

He was awake ten minutes before the alarm went off, and heard at once the light patter of rain through the open window.

'Timothy?'

---

* *The Book of Common Prayer*

'Yes?'

'Is it four o'clock?'

'Ten 'til. Go back to sleep.'

'You'll have a great time, I just know you will.'

'I'm sure of it. And remember—don't cook dinner. I'm bringing it home.'

'Right, darling. I'm excited. . . .'

She was no such thing; she was already snoring again. He kissed her shoulder and crept out of bed.

He was accustomed to rising early, but four o'clock was ridiculous, not to mention he couldn't get pumped up for this jaunt no matter how hard he tried.

He stood on the porch and drew in a deep draught of the cool morning air; it was scented with rain and salt, with something mysteriously beyond his ken. He didn't think he'd ever again take the ocean for granted. He daily sensed the power and presence of it in this new world in which they were living.

All those years ago when he was a young clergyman in a little coastal parish, the water had meant nothing to him; his mind, his heart had been elsewhere, in the clouds perhaps; but now it was different. Though he wasn't one for swimming in the ocean or broiling on the beach, he was marking a connection this time, something he couldn't quite articulate.

It was still dark when he found the marina where the charter boats were tied to the dock like horses to be saddled.

He pulled into the parking lot, took his gear from the trunk, and locked up. People were huffing coolers as big as coffins out of vans and cars, muttering, calling to each other, laughing, slamming doors.

Raining a little harder now, but nothing serious. He wiped his head with his hat and put it back in his pocket, checking his watch. Five o'clock sharp.

He hefted the cooler and started walking, looking for *Blue Heaven* and trying to get over the feeling he was still asleep and this was a dream.

Someone materialized out of the gray mist, smelling intensely of tobacco and shaving lotion.

'Mornin', Father! Let's go fishin'!'

'Otis? Is that you?'

'Cap'n Willie told me you were on board today. I didn't want you goin' off by yourself and havin' too much fun.'

A bronzed, bearded Captain Willie stood on the deck wearing shorts and a T-shirt, booming out a welcome.

'Father Timothy! Good mornin' to you, we're glad to have you!'

He found himself shaking a hand as big as a ham and hard as a rock. 'Step over lightly, now, let me take that, there you go, welcome to *Blue Heaven*.'

'Good morning, Captain. How's the weather looking?' It seemed the boat was lurching around in the water pretty good, and they hadn't even gone anywhere yet.

'Goin' to fair off and be good fishin'.' Captain Willie's genial smile displayed a couple of gold teeth. 'Meet my first mate, Pete Brady.'

He shook hands with a muscular fellow of about thirty. 'Good to see you, Pete.'

'Yessir, welcome aboard.'

'This your first time?' asked Captain Willie.

'First ever.'

'Well, you're fishin' with a pro, here.' He pounded Otis on the back. 'Go on in th' cabin, set your stuff down, make yourself at home. And Father . . .'

'Yes?'

'Would you favor us with blessin' the fleet this mornin'?'

'Ah . . . how does that work, exactly?'

'All th' boats'll head out about th' same time, then after the sun rises, you'll come up to th' bridge an' ask th' Lord for safe passage and good fishin'. Th' other boats can hear you over th' radio.'

'Consider it done!' he said, feeling a surge of excitement.

'We'll have prayer requests for you. Like, the last few days, we've all been prayin' for Cap'n Tucker's daughter, she's got leukemia.'

'I'm sorry. I'd feel honored and blessed to do it.'

'We thank you. Now go in there and introduce yourselves around, get comfortable.'

Father Tim stuck his head in the cabin.

Ernie Fulcher, sitting with a green cooler between his feet, threw up his hand and grinned from ear to ear. 'Didn't want you runnin' out th' first time all by your lonesome.'

'Right,' said Roger, looking shy about butting in. 'We didn't think you'd mind a little company.'

Madge Parrot and her friend Sybil Huffman appeared to be dressed for a cruise in the Bahamas. They were clearly proud to announce they were from Rome, Georgia, and this was their first time on a fishing charter.

Both were widows whose husbands had been great fisherman. This trip was about making a connection with the departed, as they'd heard Chuck and Roy talk about deep-sea fishing like it was the best thing since sliced bread. Madge confessed that even though she and Sybil didn't drink beer, they didn't see why they couldn't catch fish like anybody else.

He noted that the group shared a need to explain what they had in their coolers, some even lifting the lids and displaying the contents, issuing hearty invitations to dip in, at any time, to whatever they'd brought along.

'You run out of drinks, me'n Roger got all you want right here,' said Ernie, patting a cooler as big as a Buick. 'Got Sun-Drop, Mello Yello, Sprite, just help yourself.'

'And there's ham and turkey on rye,' said Roger. 'I made two extra, just in case, plus fried chicken.'

Everybody nodded their thanks, as the engines began to throb and hum. Father Tim was mum about the contents of his own cooler—two banana sandwiches on white bread with low-fat mayo.

'Y'all need any sunscreen,' said Madge, 'we're loaded with sunscreen. It's right here in my jacket pocket.' She indicated a blue jacket folded on the seat, so that one and all might note its whereabouts in an emergency.

'And I've got Bonine,' said Sybil, 'if anybody feels seasick.' She held up her package and rattled the contents.

'Have you ever been seasick?' Madge asked Father Tim.

'Never!' he said. Truth was, he'd never been on the sea but a couple of times, and always in sight of the shore, so there was no way he could have been seasick. And for today, he'd done what Ernie and Roger so heartily recommended—he'd stayed sober, gotten a good night's sleep, and didn't eat a greasy breakfast.

'Only twelve percent of people get seasick,' Roger said, quoting his most encouraging piece of information on the subject.

Ernie lifted the lid of his cooler. 'Oh, an' anybody wants Snickers bars, they're right here on top of th' ice. There's nothin' like a Snickers iced down good'n cold.'

Madge and Sybil admitted they'd never heard of icing down a Snickers bar, but thought it would be real tasty, especially on a hot day. Sybil pledged to try one before the trip was over.

Otis announced that anybody who wanted to help themselves to his Kentucky Fried, they knew where it was at. He also had cigars, Johnnie Walker Black, and boiled peanuts, for whoever took a notion.

It was the most instant formation of community Father Tim had ever witnessed. He felt momentarily inspired to stand and lead a hymn.

Captain Willie gunned the engines, and the stern of the *Blue Heaven* dug low into the water as they moved away from the dock at what seemed like full speed.

The sun was emerging from the water, staining the silver sea with patches of light and color.

Pete Brady came into the cabin, holding a dripping ballyhoo in one hand. 'You'll want to go up to the bridge now, sir. Better put your jacket on.'

'Right!' he said. He was glad to leave the cabin; only a moment ago, he'd had the odd sensation of smothering. . . .

He stood, holding onto the table that was bolted to the deck, then made his way to the door, praying he wouldn't pitch into Madge Parrott's lap.

'You tell th' Lord we're wantin' 'em to weigh fifty pounds and up, if He don't mind.' Otis chewed his cigar and grinned.

Father Tim clung to the doorjamb. 'How do I get to the bridge?' he asked Pete.

The first mate, who appeared to be squeezing the guts from a bait fish, jerked his thumb toward the side of the cabin. 'Right up the ladder there.'

He peered around and saw a ladder. The rungs were immediately over the water, and went straight up. Three, four, five . . .

'*That* ladder?'

'Yessir, be sure'n hold on tight.'

He turned and lunged for the bottom rung of the ladder, but miscalculated and bounced onto the rail. Too startled to grab hold, he reeled against the cabin wall, finally managing to grip the lower rung. Thanks be to God, Pete was baiting a hook and facing seaward, and his cabin mates were oblivious to his afflictions.

Lord Jesus, I've never done this before. You were plenty good around water, and I'm counting on You to help me accomplish this thing.

He reached for an upper rung and got a firm grip. He swung himself onto the ladder and went up, trying in vain to curl his tennis shoes around the rungs like buns around frankfurters.

He hauled himself to the bridge, grabbed the support rail for the hard top, and stood for a moment, awed. The view from the bridge literally took his breath away.

How could anyone doubt the living truth of what the psalmist said? *'The heavens declare the glory of God, the skies proclaim the work of his hands!'* He wanted to shout in unabashed praise.

Surely this was the habitation of angels, and life in the cabin a thing to be pitied.

He lurched to the helm, where Captain Willie was holding a microphone, and grabbed the back of the helm chair.

'We're glad to have you with us, Father! Greetings to you from th' whole fleet on this beautiful September day!'

His stomach did an odd turn as he opened his mouth to speak, so he closed it again.

The captain winked. 'Got a little chop this mornin'. A real sharp head sea.'

He felt sweat on his brow as the captain spoke into the microphone.

'We're mighty happy to have Father Tim Kavanagh to lead us in prayer this mornin'. He's from over at Whitecap. Anybody with a prayer request, let's hear it now.'

The VHF blared. 'Father, my little boy fell off a ladder on Sunday, he's, ah, in the hospital, looks like he's goin' to be fine but . . . his name's Danny. We thank you.'

'Please pray for Romaine, he had his leg tore up. A tractor fell on 'im. Thank you.'

'Just like to ask for . . . forgiveness for somethin' I done, there's no use to go into what, I'd appreciate it.'

Several other requests came in as he bent his head and listened intently, gripping the helm chair for all he was worth.

'That's it? Anybody else?'

Then he took the microphone, surprised that it felt as heavy as a lug wrench.

'We'd like to pray for th' owner of th' marina and his wife, Angie, too,' said Captain Willie. 'She's got breast cancer. And Cap'n Tucker's daughter, we don't want to forget her, name's Sarah, then there's Toby Rider, lost his daddy and we feel real bad about it. Course we'd like to ask God's mercy for every family back home and every soul on board. . . .'

Captain Willie turned to the helm, grabbed the red knob, and cranked the engines back to idle.

In the sudden quiet, the waves slammed against the hull, dulling the gurgling sound of the exhaust. They seemed to be wallowing now in the choppy sea; they might have been so much laundry tossing in a washing machine.

His heart was hammering as if he'd run a race. But it wasn't his heart, exactly, that bothered him, it was his stomach. It seemed strangely disoriented, as if it had moved to a new location and he couldn't figure out where.

'Our Father, we thank You mightily for the beauty of the sunrise over this vast sea, and for the awe and wonder in all the gifts of Your creation. We ask Your generous blessings upon every captain and mate aboard every vessel in this fleet, and pray that each of us be made able, by Your grace, to know Your guidance, love, and mercy throughout the day. . . .'

The names of the people, and their needs, what were they? His mind seemed desperately blank, as if every shred of thought and reason had been blown away like chaff on the wind.

Lord! Help!

'For Sarah, we ask Your tender mercies, that You would keep her daily in Your healing care, giving wisdom to those attending her, and providing strength and encouragement. . . .'

More than three decades of intercessory prayer experience notwithstanding, he found it miraculous that the names came to him, one by one. He leaned into the prayer with intensity, feeling something of the genuine weight and burden, the urgency, of the needs for which he prayed.

He wiped the sweat from his forehead. 'Oh, Lord, who maketh a way in the sea, and a path in the mighty waters, we thank You for hearing our prayers, in the blessed name of Your Son, our Savior, Jesus Christ. Amen.'

The captain took the microphone and keyed it, thanking him.

He noted what appeared to be a look of compassion on the captain's face as they shook hands.

'*Blue Heaven*, *Salty Dog*, come back.'

'*Blue Heaven*, go ahead, *Salty Dog*.'

'Just want to say we really appreciate Father Kavanagh's prayers, and sure hope he doesn't succumb to the torments of a rough sea. OK, *Salty Dog* back to eighty.'

As the captain gunned the engines, Father Tim careened to the rail and leaned over.

The goodwill and fond hope of the *Salty Dog* had come too late.

Twice over the rail should nip this thing in the bud. Already his ribs hurt from retching; it was probably over now and he could go down the ladder and have something to drink, maybe even a bite to eat— that was the problem, going out on rough seas with an empty stomach. . . .

Good grief! He scrambled off the ladder and leaned over the rail, the bile spewing in a flume from his very core, hot, bitter, and fathomless.

Conversations came and went; it was all a kind of hive hum, he thought, as when bees returned from working a stand of sourwoods.

'Now, you take the tarpon,' said Otis. 'I was down in th' Keys where they grow too big to mount on your wall. Tarpon you just jump a few times and then break 'em off before you wear 'em out, you wear 'em out too bad, th' sharks eat 'em.'

'I never fished any tarpon,' said Ernie.

'See you pop th' eyes out like this . . . then you break up th' backbone . . .'

'Oooh,' said Madge.

'Don't make 'er faint,' said Otis.

'I have no intention of fainting, thank you!'

'Then you squeeze their guts out, see . . .'

'Lord help,' said Sybil.

'Thing is, th' more they wiggle in th' water, th' better they catch.'

'Clever!' said Madge. 'That is *really* clever.'

Without realizing how he got there, he was at the rail again, on his knees.

'On his knees at th' rail,' said Madge. 'That is very Episcopalian.'

'Or Luth'ran,' said Sybil. 'Can't that be Luth'ran?'

He didn't know who it was, Otis or Ernie, but someone held his head while he spewed up his insides and watched the vomitus carried away on the lashing water.

'We been out every day for forty-one days straight,' said Pete, who was currently varying the bait, trying anything.

'Sometimes you just pray for a nor'easter so you can get a break, but if th' weather's good, you have to go.'

The weather today is not *good*, he tried to say, but couldn't. Why in blazes did we go today if you don't go when the weather's not good? *Answer that!*

He was baking, he was broiling, he was frying, he was cooked. He remembered the sunscreen in his jacket pocket, but he wasn't wearing his jacket. Someone had helped him remove it earlier.

'Look,' said Sybil. 'Th' poor man needs something.'

'Here you go,' Otis was patting sunscreen on his head and followed it with a hat.

'Bless you,' he managed to whisper.

'What'd he say?'

'He said bless me.' He thought Otis sounded touched. 'Father, you want some water or Coke? Coke might be good.'

'Nossir,' said Ernie, 'what he needs is ginger ale. Anybody got ginger ale?'

'Fruit juice,' said Madge, 'that's what I'd give somebody with upset stomach.'

'No deal with th' fruit juice,' said Pete. 'Too much acid.'

'How about a piece of ice just to hold in his mouth?'

'I don't know about that. They say when you're real hot you shouldn't swallow somethin' real cold, it can give you a heart attack or maybe a stroke.'

'He's moving his lips. What's he saying?'

Otis leaned down and listened. 'He's praying,' said Otis.

He was shocked to find himself kneeling at the rail again, with no power over this thing, none at all. He might have been a piece of bait himself, without will or reason to alter his circumstances.

'Number five,' somebody said. 'That's th' fifth time.'

'Seven. He heaved over th' bridge rail twice.'

'You ready to eat? I'm half starved.'

'I've been thinkin' about what I made last night. Tuna salad. On French bread! Oh, and there's late tomatoes out of my neighbor's garden. Delicious!' said Madge. 'I'll cut 'em up so we can all have a bite.'

'Tuna out of a *can?*' asked Otis. 'That'd be sacreligious.'

'Are we goin' to just leave 'im out here?' wondered Sybil.

'Father? *Father!*'

Why did people think the sick automatically went deaf?

What? He couldn't say it audibly, so he thought it, which should be sufficient.

'Do you want to go inside?'

'Don't take him inside,' said the first mate. 'You lose th' horizon when you do that. That's usually what makes people seasick, is losin' th' horizon.'

'But he's been sittin' out here since it quit rainin'. I think we should at least put sunscreen on his arms. Look at his arms.'

He felt several people pawing over him, and tried to express his gratitude.

'Lookit. He doesn't have socks on. Rub some on his ankles.'

'Th' back of his neck,' said Ernie. 'That's a real tender place, slather some on there.'

'He's an *awful* color,' said Madge.

He realized he should have been more specific in his will; now it was too late to say that he did *not* want an open casket.

Thank God! He might actually be feeling better.

His eyes seemed clear, some strength was returning; but he didn't want to count his chickens, no, indeed. He rubbed

ChapStick on his lips and hunkered down under Otis's hat, wondering about his sugar, which must have dropped straight to the floor of the Gulf Stream. He wished he'd brought his tachometer . . . no, that wasn't it. What was it, anyway? Could he have possibly suffered brain damage from this terrible assault? *Glu*cometer, that's what it was.

Weak . . . terribly weak. He realized he was thinking of Ernie's Snickers bars, iced down cold. A small flicker, a flame of hope rose in his breast. *Thank you, Lord. . . .*

Father Tim waved his hand to Ernie, who came over and squatted by the chair.

'What can I do for you, buddy?'

'Snickers,' he said, hoarse as a bullfrog.

'Snickers?'

He nodded, feeble but encouraged.

'We got us one!' yelled Ernie. 'Otis! Where's Otis?'

'In th' head. You take it!'

Father Tim had heard of total pandemonium, but he'd never seen it 'til now. Six people erupted into a full horde, and swarmed around him like the armies of Solomon.

'We got a fish here! Yee-hah!'

He looked at the throbbing lines crisscrossed over and around the stern like freeways through L.A.

'That's a keeper!' Pete gaffed something and pulled it in.

'Way to go, Roger!'

He saw the rainbow of color that shimmered on the big fish as it went into the box, where it thrashed like a horse kicking a stall. Pete pulled out the gaff and hosed blood from the deck.

The captain was fishing off the bridge; everybody was fishing. He heaved himself from the chair, out of the fray, and huddled against the cabin.

In the fighting chair, Madge was crouched into the labor of hauling in something big.

Otis had his thumb on her line, helping her raise and lower the rod. 'You got to pump 'im now,' he said, clenching his cigar in his teeth.

'Oh, law! This much be an eighteen-wheeler I've got on here!'

'Keep crankin'!'

Captain Willie called over the speaker, 'Please tend to the left-hand corner, Pete, tend to the left-hand corner, we got a mess over there.'

'A fishin' frenzy,' muttered Pete, streaking by in a blur.

Madge cranked the reel, blowing like a prizefighter. 'This fish is killin' me. Somebody come and take this bloomin' rod!'

'Don't quit!' yelled Sybil, aiming a point-and-shoot at the action. 'Keep goin', Chuck would be so proud!'

'That ain't nothin' but solid tuna,' said Otis. He helped Madge lift the rod as the fish drew closer to the boat.

Father Tim rubberlegged it to the stern and looked over. The black water of morning had changed to blue-green, and the fish moved beneath the surface, luminous and quick.

He thought it one of the most beautiful sights he'd ever seen.

'Here it comes!'

He stepped back as Pete darted to the right of the fighting chair, lowered the gaff, and hauled the tuna onto the deck.

'Way to go, Madge!'

'Beautiful! *Beautiful!*'

Whistles, cheers, applause.

'That'll weigh in seventy, seventy-five pounds,' Otis said, as Madge staggered out of the chair, grinning into Sybil's camera.

The captain was catching fish, Ernie was catching fish, Roger was catching fish.

'Got a fish on th' line!' yelled Peter. 'Who'll take it?'

'I'll take it!' As Father Tim thumped into the fighting chair, hoots of encouragement went up from the entire assembly.

He was back from the dead, he was among the living, he was ready to do this thing.

'How was it, darling?'

'Terrific!' he said, kissing her. 'Wonderful fellowship, *great* fellowship—fellows in a ship, get it?'

'Got it. And the weather?'

He shrugged. 'A little rough, but not too bad.'

'What's for supper?' she asked, eyeing the cooler he was lugging.

'Yellowfin tuna and dolphin! Let's fire up the grill,' he said, trotting down the hall, 'and I'll tell you all about it!' By the time he hit the deck, he was whistling.

She hurried after her husband, feeling pleased. He'd come home looking considerably thinner, definitely tanner, and clearly more relaxed. She'd known all along that buying him a chair with Captain Willie was a brilliant idea.

—Chapter 13
Mighty Waters

One of the most compelling characters who has walked into a Mitford novel is Morris Love, a genius with all the torment that can come with a brilliant mind and creative soul.

He would not exhort God this morning to heal, bind up, or transform. He would exhort Him only to bless.

He prayed, silent.

Bless the gift You have given Morris Love, to be used to Your glory, bless his spirit which craves You and yet bids You not enter, bless the laughter that is surely there, laughter that has dwelled in him all these years, yearning to be released, longing to spring forth and be a blessing to others. . . .

The laughter of Morris Love—that would be a miracle, he thought, and remembered how he had prayed to hear Dooley Barlowe laugh. That prayer had been answered; he smiled to think of Dooley's riotous cackle.

Thank You for blessing Morris with a quick and lively mind, an inquisitive intellect, and a soul able to perform music which ardently glorifies the Giver. Thank You for blessing Morris with Mamie, who, out of all those offered the glad opportunity of loving him, was the only one who came forth to love and serve on Your behalf.

Lord, bless him today as he sits at his keyboard, as he breaks bread with Mamie, as he looks out his window onto a world that betrayed him, and that he now betrays. As he lies down to sleep, bless him with Your holy peace. As he rises, bless him with hope. As he thinks, bless him with Your own high thoughts.

Now, Father, I bless You—and praise You and thank You for

*hearing my prayer, through Christ our Lord who was given to us that
we might have new life, Amen.*

—Chapter 21
True Confessions

And then the storm came to Whitecap, and to the fragile,
historic church building of St. John's in the Grove. After the
long siege of repairs and restoration, the parish comes together
to celebrate.

'When trees and power lines crashed around you, when the very roof
gave way above you, when light turned to darkness and water turned
to dust, did you call on Him?

'When you called on Him, was He somewhere up there, or was
He as near as your very breath?'

He stood in front of the pulpit this morning, looking into the
faces of those whom God had given into his hands for this brief moment in time.

'What some believers still can't believe is that it is God's passion
to be as near to us as our very breath.

'Far more than I want us to have a bigger crowd or a larger parish
hall or a more ambitious budget . . . more than anything as your
priest, I pray for each and every one of you to sense and know God's
presence . . . as near as your breath.

'In short, it has been my prayer since we came here for you to
have a personal, one-on-one, day-to-day relationship with Christ.

'I'm talking about something that goes beyond every Sunday service ever created or ever to be created, something you can depend on

for the rest of your life, and then forever. I'm talking about the times you cry out in the storm that prevails against you, times when your heart and your flesh fail and you see no way out and no way in, when any prayer you utter to a God you may view as distant and disinterested seems to vanish into thin air.

'There are legions who believe in the existence of a cold and distant God, and on the occasions when they cry out to Him in utter despair and hear nothing in reply, must get up and stumble on, alone.

'Then there are those who know Him personally, who have found that when they cry out, there He is, as near as their breath—one-on-one, heart-to-heart, savior, Lord, partner, friend.

'Some have been in church all their lives and have never known this marvelous, yet simple personal relationship. Others believe that while such a relationship may be possible, it's not for them—why would God want to bother with them, except from a very great distance? In reality, it is no bother to God at all. He wants this relationship far more than you and I want it, and I pray that you will ponder that mighty truth.

'But who among us could ever deserve to have such an altogether unimaginable thing as a close, personal, day-to-day relationship with Almighty God, creator of the universe?

'It seems unthinkable, and so . . . we are afraid to think it.

'For this designated time in history, this tender and fleeting moment of our lives, I am your priest; God has called me to lead this flock. As I look out this morning, my heart has a wish list for you. For healed marriages, good jobs, the well-being and safety of your children; on and on, there are fervent desires upon my heart for you. But chief among the hopes, the prayers, the petition is this: *Lord . . . let my people know.* Let them know that the unthinkable is not only real, but available and possible and can be entered into, now, today—though we are, indeed, completely undeserving.

'It can be entered into today, with only a simple prayer that some think not sophisticated enough to bring them into the presence of God. . . .

'Yet, this prayer makes it possible for you to know Him not only as Savior and Lord, but as a friend. "*No longer do I call you servants*," He said to His followers in the Gospel of John, '"*but friends.*"

'In the storms of your life, do you long for the consolation of His nearness and His friendship? You can't imagine how He longs for the consolation of yours. It is unimaginable, isn't it, that He would want to be near us—frail as we are, weak as we are, and hopeless as we so often feel. God wants to be *with us*. That, in fact, is His name: Immanuel, God with us. And why is that so hard to imagine, when indeed, He made us for Himself? Please hear that this morning. The One who made us . . . made us for Himself.

'There are some of you who want to be done with seeking Him once a week, and crave, instead, to be with Him day after day, telling him everything, letting it all hang out, just thankful to have such a blessing in your life as a friend who will never, under any circumstances, leave you, and never remove His love from you. Amazing? Yes, it is. It is amazing.

'We're reminded in the Book of Revelation that He created all things—for His pleasure. Many of us believe that He created all things, but we forget the very best part—that He created us . . . *for His pleasure.*

'God knows who is longing to utter that simple prayer this morning. It is a matter between you and Him, and it is a prayer which will usher you into His presence, into life everlasting, and into the intimacy of a friendship in which He is as near . . . as your breath.

'Here's the way this wondrous prayer works—as you ask Him into your heart, He receives you into His. The heart of God! What a place to be, to reside for eternity.

'As we bow our heads to pray under this new roof and inside these new walls, I ask that He graciously bless each and every one of us today . . . with new hearts.

'Sense, feel God's presence among us this morning . . .'

He waited.

'. . . as those of you who are moved to do so, silently repeat this simple prayer:

'Thank You, God, for loving me . . .

'. . . and for sending Your Son to die for my sins.

'I sincerely repent of my sins . . .

'. . . and receive Jesus Christ as my personal savior.

'Now, as Your child . . .

'. . . I turn my entire life over to You.

'Amen.'

—Chapter 22
A New Song

I have called you by name—you are mine.

—Isaiah 43:1

I will give you the treasures of darkness, riches stored in secret places, so that you may know that I am the Lord, the God of Israel, who summons you by name.

—Isaiah 45:3

A COMMON LIFE

When *A Common Life* hit the street, it also hit at number one on the *New York Times* and other bestseller lists. The fifth novel was something of an oddity, really, because it took readers back in time to Father Tim and Cynthia's wedding. At that point in the series, they had already been married for several years. So how could this happen?

It happened because Mitford fans, even at this late date, still begged for the missing details of the proposal, the engagement period, and the wedding.

Therefore, some now read *A Common Life* as number five and others choose to read it in the number three slot, following the marriage banns published at the end of the previous novel, *A Light in the Window*. Confusing? You bet. And also a lot of fun, thanks to Father Tim's bachelor anxieties, Cynthia's late arrival at the ceremony, and the parish's reaction to the miraculous news.

No wonder he had counseled so many men before their walk down the aisle; the true softening of the heart and spirit toward a woman was usually an alarmingly unfamiliar feeling. How might a man wield a spear and shield, preserve his very life, if he were poured out at her feet like so much pudding?

He turned off the lamp and prayed aloud in the dark room.

'Father, we bless You and thank You for this miracle, for choosing us to receive it.

'May we treat the love You've given us with gratitude and devotion, humor and astonishment.

'May it be a river of living water to bring delight and encouragement to others, Lord, for we must never hold this rare blessing to ourselves, but pour it out like wine.

'Protect her, Lord, give her courage for whatever lies ahead, and give me, I pray, whatever is required to love her well and steadfastly all the days of our lives.'

There was something else, something else to be spoken tonight. He was quiet for a time in the still, dark room where only the sound of his dog's snoring was heard.

Yes. There it was. The old and heavy thing he so often ignored, that needed to be said.

'Father—continue to open me and lay me bare, for I have been selfish and closed, always keeping something back, even from You. Forgive me. . . .'

The clock ticked.

The curtains blew out in a light breeze.

'Through Jesus Christ, our Lord.

'Amen.'

—Chapter 2
The Grill

'Tell me,' he said at last. 'Tell me everything. I'm your priest, after all.'

She thought his smile dazzling, a dazzling thing to come out of quietude. She had pulled a footstool to the love seat and sat close to him.

'I'm afraid I can't make you happy,' she said.

'But that was my fear. I finally kicked it out the back door and now it's run over here.'

'It's not funny, Timothy.'

'I'm not laughing.'

He took her hands in his and lightly kissed the tips of her fingers and she caught the scent of him, the innocence of him, and her spirit mounted up again.

'Why don't we pray together?' he said. 'Just let our hearts speak to His. . . .'

She bowed her head and closed her eyes and he stroked her shoulder. Though the clock ticked in the hallway, she supposed that time was standing still, and that she might sit with him in this holy reverie forever.

'Lord,' he said, simply, 'here we are.'

'Yes, Lord, here we are.'

They drew in their breath as one, and let it out in a long sigh, and she realized for a moment how the very act of breathing in His presence was a balm.

'Dear God,' he said, 'deliver Your cherished one from feeling helpless to receive the love You give so freely from the depths of Your being. Help us to be as large as the love You've given us; sometimes it's too great for us, Lord, even painful. Tear away the old fears, the old boundaries that no longer contain anything of worth or importance, and by Your grace, make Cynthia able to seize the bold, fresh freedom. . . .'

'Yes, Lord,' she prayed, 'the freedom I've never really known before, but which You've faithfully shown me in glimmers, in epiphanies, in wisps as fragile as light from Your new moon.'

He pressed her hand, feeling in it the beating of her pulse.

'Father, deliver me from the fear to love wholly and completely, I who chided this good man for his own fears, his own weakness, while posing, without knowing it a pose, as confident and bold. You've seen through that, Lord, You've found me out for what I am . . .'

There was a long silence, filled by the ticking of the clock.

'. . . a frightened seven-year-old who stands at the door looking for a father and mother who . . . do not come home.

'Even after years of knowing You as a Father who is always home, I sometimes feel—I feel a prisoner of old and wrenching fears, and I'm ashamed of my fear, and the darkness that prevents me from stepping into the light. . . .'

'You tell us in Your Word,' he prayed, 'that You do not give us the spirit of fear—'

'But of power and of love and a sound mind!' she whispered.

'And so, Lord, I rebuke the Enemy who would employ every strategy to deny Your children the blessing of Your grace.'

'Yes, Lord!'

'Help us to receive Your peace and courage, Your confidence and power,' he said.

'And Father,' she said, 'please give me the grace to love Dooley as You love him, and the patience to encourage and support and understand him, for I wish with all my heart that we might grow together as a true family.' She took a deep and satisfying breath. 'And now, Lord . . .'

As the prayer neared its end, they spoke in unison as they had recently begun to do in their evening prayers.

'. . . create in us a clean heart . . . renew a right spirit within us . . . and fill us with Your Holy Spirit . . . through Christ our Lord . . . amen.'

He helped her from the footstool and she sat beside him on the love seat and breathed the peace that settled over them like a shawl.

'There will be many times when fear breaks in,' he said, holding her close. 'We can never be taken prisoner if we greet it with prayer.'

—Chapter 7
The Prayer

· ≫ ✽ ≪ ·

Dooley is preparing to sing for Father Tim and Cynthia at their wedding.

Dooley sat on the side of his bed and felt a creeping, lopsided nausea that came with the aroma of baked ham as it rose from the kitchen. He said three four-letter words in a row, and was disappointed when his stomach still felt sick.

He hoped his voice wouldn't crack during the hymn. Though he'd agreed to sing a cappella, he didn't trust a cappella. If you hit a wrong note, there was nothing to cover you. He wished there were trumpets or something really loud behind him, but no, Cynthia wanted 'Dooley's pure singing voice.' Gag.

'God,' he said aloud, 'don't let me sound weird. Amen.' He had no idea that God would really hear him or prevent him from sounding weird, but he thought it was a good idea to ask.

—Chapter 8
The Preamble

At precisely five o'clock, Father Tim heard the organ. What was going on? Why hadn't anyone come to the outer sacristy door to tell them the bride had arrived?

'Don't go out there!' he nearly shouted, as the bishop's hand went for the door that led to the sanctuary. 'Walter, please find Katherine, find out what's going on.' Somebody had missed a signal.

At five after five, Walter reappeared, looking mystified. 'Katherine can't find Cynthia. She was supposed to meet her in the narthex at five 'til.'

Ten minutes late! Cynthia Coppersmith was the very soul of punctuality.

He had a gut feeling, and it wasn't good. 'I'll be back,' he said, sprinting through the open door.

He dashed up Old Church Lane, cut through Baxter Park, and hit her back steps running.

'Cynthia!' He was trembling as he opened the unlocked door and ran into the hall.

He took the stairs two at a time and hung a left into her bedroom. 'Cynthia!'

'Timothy!'

She was beating on her bathroom door from the inside. 'Timothy! I can't get out!'

He spied the blasted doorknob lying on the floor. He picked it up and stuck the stem back in the hole and cranked the knob to the right and the door opened and he saw his bride in her chenille robe and pink curlers, looking agonized.

'Oh, Timothy . . .'

'Don't talk,' he said. 'Don't even tell me. How can I help you, what can I do?'

She raced to the closet and took out her suit. 'Stand outside and I'll do my best. Pray for me, darling! Oh, I'm so sorry, I should have borrowed something blue for good luck, what a dreadful mess . . .'

He stood in the hall and checked his watch. Five-seventeen.

'Oh dreadful, oh horrid!' she cried, finishing her mascara with a shaking hand. 'And I just remembered, you're not supposed to see the bride before the ceremony!'

She got up and dashed toward him.

'Curlers,' he said, jaws cranking still further into the lock position. 'Rats!'

She plucked the curlers from her head like so many feathers from a chick, and tossed them into the air. They literally rained around the room.

'No time to brush!' She looked into the mirror and ran her fingers through her hair. 'There! Best I can do. God help me!'

She turned to him now, and he felt a great jolt from heart to spleen. She was so astonishingly beautiful, so radiant, so fresh, it captured his very breath. Thanks be to God, his custard was back. . . .

She grabbed her handbag from the chair. 'We can take my car!'

'No place to park!'

'So,' she cried, as they headed for the stairs, 'race you!'

—Chapter 8
The Preamble

Father Tim took Cynthia's right hand in his, and carefully spoke the words he never imagined might be his own.

'In the name of God, I, Timothy, take you, Cynthia, to be my wife, to have and to hold from this day forward, for better for worse, for richer for poorer, in sickness and in health, to love and to cherish, until we are parted by death.

'This is my solemn vow.'

They loosed their hands for a moment, a slight movement that caused the candle flames on the altar to tremble. Then she took his right hand in hers.

'In the name of God, I, Cynthia, take you, Timothy, to be my husband, to have and to hold from this day forward, for better for worse, for richer for poorer, in sickness and in health, to love and to cherish, until we are parted by death.

'This is my solemn vow.'

As Walter presented the ring to the groom, the bishop raised his right hand. 'Bless, O Lord, these rings to be a sign of the vows by which this man and this woman have bound themselves to each other; through Jesus Christ our Lord, Amen.'

'Cynthia, I give you this ring as a symbol of my vow, and with all that I am, and all that I have, I honor you in the name of the Father, and of the Son, and of the Holy Spirit.'

She felt the worn gold ring slipping on her finger; it seemed weightless, a band of silk.

Katherine stepped forward then, delivering the heavy gold band with the minuscule engraving upon its inner circle: *Until heaven and then forever.*

'Timothy . . . I give you this ring as a symbol of my vow, and with all that I am, and all that I have, I honor you, in the name of the Father, and of the Son, and of the Holy Spirit.'

Hessie Mahew was convinced the bishop looked right into her eyes as he spoke.

'Now that Cynthia and Timothy have given themselves to each other by solemn vows, with the joining of hands and the giving and receiving of rings, I pronounce that they are husband and wife, in the name of the Father, and of the Son, and of the Holy Spirit.

'Those whom God has joined together . . . let no man put asunder.'*

—Chapter 9
The Wedding

---

* *The Book of Common Prayer,* The Celebration and Blessing of a Marriage

I don't want so much of your money and so much of your work. I want you . . . I don't want to cut off a branch here and a branch there, I want to have the whole tree down . . . Hand over the natural self, all the desires which you think innocent as well as the ones you think wicked—the whole outfit. I will give you a new self instead. I will give you Myself: my own will shall become yours.

—C.S. Lewis, *The Joyful Christian*
Patches of Godlight: Father Tim's Favorite Quotes

IN THIS MOUNTAIN

Cynthia and Father Tim have returned to Mitford from a year at St. John's in Whitecap. Father Tim is conflicted—again about retirement. They decide to join a ministry in Tennessee, but before they can get there, he is involved in a terrible accident that affects his health, his marriage, and the whole town. As he struggles to forgive himself, he is pounded by a deep depression. It's a time of darkness for a man who brings light into the lives of so many.

"*"O Lord, You are my portion and my cup . . . ,"*" he recited in unison with Cynthia and the other parishioners. "*"It is You who uphold my lot. My boundaries enclose a pleasant land; indeed, I have a goodly heritage. I will bless the Lord Who gives me counsel; my heart teaches me, night after night. I have set the Lord always before me; because He is at my right hand I shall not fall. "*"*

---

* Psalm 16:5–11

Cynthia slipped her arm around him as they shared the Psalter. *"'My heart, therefore, is glad, and my spirit rejoices; my body also shall rest in hope. For You will not abandon me to the grave, nor let Your holy one see the pit."*

"'You will show me the path of life; in Your presence there is fullness of joy, and in Your right hand are pleasures for evermore.'"

His heart was warmed by the familiar words, words he had memorized—when? Had he been ten years old, or twelve?

He looked at his wife and was moved by a certain tenderness. The boy who had recited those words before a hushed Sunday school class in Holly Springs, Mississippi—what a miracle that he was standing now in Wesley, North Carolina, more than half a century later, knowing a simple happiness he'd never hoped to experience.

—Chapter 1
Go and Tell

Let's be grateful that prayer can happen anywhere, anytime. In a bookstore. In an email. On the phone. At the checkout counter. The power—and peace—of it is available 24/7.

'A few weeks ago,' said Hope Winchester, 'Helen asked me to hire part-time help to take care of our mail order for the rare books. Without considering the circumstances, I hired George. I know she trusts me completely, I've never let her down.

'Now I don't know what to do. George Gaynor has a criminal record.'

'St. Paul asked us to be instant in prayer. Don't be alarmed, but I'm going to pray about this right now.'

'Right *now*?' said Hope.

He bowed his head. 'Father, we're in a pickle here. Thank You for giving Hope wisdom about what to do and putting Your answer plainly in her heart. In Jesus' name, amen.'

Hope looked at him quizzically. 'Is that all?'

'That's it!' he said. 'Just check your heart, you'll know what to do.'

'Oh,' she said, oddly relieved.

'And by the way, I think everyone will love George Gaynor all over again.'

—Chapter 4
www.seek&find.com

⁂

'Let me pray for us,' he said, smoothing her hair from her forehead. The faintest scent of wisteria rose from her flesh, evanescent but consoling. He'd be able to locate his wife anywhere; her scent had become the smell of home to him.

'Lord,' he said, 'to You all hearts are open, all desires known, and from You no secrets are hid. We can hide nothing from You, yet something is hidden from us. Speak to us again, Father, help us discern Your direction for our lives. Are we on the path you've set for us? Have we missed the mark?'

They lay still then, hearing the ticking of the clock, and Barnabas snoring on the hall landing.

—Chapter 5
A Sudden Darkness

·⟶⟶⟶⟶·

He has fanned the fire of his diabetes and sunk into the second coma of his life, following a car accident in which he injured a fellow pastor and killed the man's beloved dog.

A voice murmured at his right ear; he felt a warm breath that cosseted his hearing and made it acute.

'O God, Light of lights, Keep us from the inward darkness. Grant us so to sleep in peace, that we may arise to work according to Your will.'*

The voice ceased, and he waited to hear it again, desperately wished to hear it again. *Is that all?* There came a kind of whirring in his head, as of planets turning, and then the voice warmed his ear again. 'Good night, dearest. I love you more than life . . .'

He could not open his mouth, it was as if he had no mouth, only ears to catch this lovely sound, this breath as warm as the tropical isles he would never visit. Nor had he eyes to see; he discovered this when he tried to open them. No mouth to speak, no eyes to see; all he could locate was his right and waiting ear.

He tried to remember what the voice had just said to him, but could not. Speak to me again! he cried from his heart. *Please!* But he heard nothing more.

—Chapter 6
The Vale

---

* *The Book of Common Prayer*

The sound of birdsong was sharp and clear, the sky cloudless. He was walking along a woodland trail, carrying something on his back. He supposed it might be a pack, but he didn't check to see. In trying to position the thing between the blades of his aching shoulders, he felt the weight shift wildly so that he lost his balance. He stumbled; the edge of the woodland path crumbled under his right foot and he fell to his knees, hard, and woke shouting.

Lord! Where are you?

He knew he had shouted, yet he hadn't heard his own voice.

The room—was it a room?—was utterly dark, and the dream—was it a dream?—had been so powerful, so convincing, that he dared not let it go. Where are You? he repeated, whispering, urgent.

Here I am, Timothy.

He lifted his hand and reached out to the Christ, whom he couldn't see but now strongly sensed to be near.

The tears were hot on his face. He had found the Lord from whom he thought himself lost, and lay back, gasping, as if he'd walked a long section of the Appalachian Trail.

Thank you! he said into the silence. Had he spoken?

"'And yea, though I walk through the valley of the shadow of death . . .'"

There was the voice at his ear, and the soft warm breath. *Stay! Don't go, don't leave me.*

"'I will fear no evil, for Thou art with me, Thy rod and Thy staff, they comfort me . . . .'"

He listened, but couldn't contain the words; he forgot them the moment they were spoken.

'I love you, my darling, my dearest, my Timothy.'

A fragrance suffused the air around his pillow, and he entered into it as if into a garden. It possessed a living and deeply familiar presence, and was something like . . .

. . . Home. But what was Home? He couldn't remember. His heart repeated the word, *Home, Home,* but his brain couldn't fathom the meaning.

—Chapter 6
The Vale

O Lord, you are my portion and my cup; it is you who upholds my lot. My boundaries enclose a pleasant land; indeed, I have a goodly heritage. I will bless the Lord who gives me counsel; my heart teaches me, night after night . . .

He stood before his Sunday school class in his mother's Baptist church and recited the whole of the Sixteenth Psalm, for which he would be given a coveted gold star to wear on his lapel.

I have set the Lord always before me; because he is at my right hand I shall not fall. My heart, therefore, is glad, and my spirit rejoices; my body also shall rest in hope. . . .

You will show me the path of life; in your presence there is fullness of joy, and in your right hand are pleasures for evermore.*

For evermore . . . the phrase moved him deeply and set him wondering about eternity and the souls of others.

---

* Psalms 16:5–11

Well done, Timothy.

Thank you, ma'am.

His heart pounded. He suddenly knew that tonight, possibly even before, he would pray, *Lord, show me the path of my life . . .*

—Chapter 6
The Vale

He sat in the pool of lamplight at three in the morning, Barnabas at his feet. He was praying the Psalms, as he'd done in times past, with the enemies of King David translated into his own enemies of fear, remorse, and self-loathing, which, in their legions, had become as armies of darkness.

Save me, O God; for the waters are come in unto my soul.

I sink in deep mire, where there is no standing: I am come into deep waters, where the floods overflow me.

I am weary of my crying: my throat is dried: mine eyes fail while I wait for my God. . . .

O God, thou knowest my foolishness; and my sins are not hid from thee. . . .

My prayer is unto thee, O Lord, in an acceptable time: O God, in the multitude of thy mercy hear me. . . .

Hear me, O Lord; for thy lovingkindness is good: turn unto me according to the multitude of thy tender mercies.

And hide not thy face from thy servant; for I am in trouble: hear me speedily.

Thou hast known my reproach, and my shame, and my dishonor: mine adversaries are all before thee.

Pour out thine indignation upon them, and let thy wrathful anger take hold of them . . . *

—Chapter 8
Tender Mercies

He'd read Paul's two epistles to Timothy on almost every birthday since his twelfth year. His mother had instructed him in this habit, and as a serious youngster, he imagined the letter to have been written across the centuries directly to him, Timothy Kavanagh. He still believed this to be true in some supernatural way.

He read aloud, knowing his dog would listen.

"'. . . continue in what you have learned and firmly believed, knowing from whom you learned it, and how from childhood you have known the sacred writings that are able to instruct you for salvation through faith in Christ Jesus.

"'. . . always be sober, endure suffering, do the work of an evangelist, carry out your ministry fully . . .'"

Carry out your ministry fully. This was the line that, every year, stopped him cold—was he carrying out his ministry fully? A few times in his priesthood he'd actually believed that he was. Now, of course, things were different.

He could journey no further with Paul tonight. Recently, he'd become aware that he was looking for something in the Scriptures. He felt desperate for a specific message from God, yet he didn't know what it might be. He knew only that it would be direct, meant profoundly for him, and that he'd recognize it when it was revealed.

---

* Psalm 69:1–24

He thumbed the Scriptures in reverse order to the voice of David, a voice in Psalm 102 that might have been his own:

'Hear my prayer, O Lord, and let my cry come unto thee.

'Hide not thy face from me in the day when I am in trouble; incline thine ear unto me: in the day when I call answer me speedily. For my days are consumed like smoke, and my bones are burned as an hearth.

'My heart is smitten, and withered like grass; so that I forget to eat my bread.

'By reason of the voice of my groaning my bones cleave to my skin.

'I am like a pelican of the wilderness: I am like an owl of the desert.

'I watch, and am as a sparrow alone upon the house top.

'My days are like a shadow that declineth; and I am withered like grass.'

—Chapter 9
Touching God

Who was to say that Cynthia wouldn't give up on him? How long could a bright, successful, beautiful woman be patient with a man who had no passion in him anywhere? His wife was all about passion; passion for whatever she was doing, for whatever lay ahead. At the beginning, she'd declared him charming and romantic—perhaps now she was changing her mind. But he couldn't bear such thoughts, it was blasphemy to think these vile things.

'Are you there? Sometimes I can't sense Your Presence, I have to go on faith alone. You want us to walk by faith, You tell us so . . . don't we go on faith that the sun will set, the moon will rise, our breath will come in and go out again, our hearts will beat? Give me faith, Lord, to know Your Presence as surely as I know the beating of my own heart. I've felt so far from You. . . .'

His life seemed overwhelmed by darkness these last weeks; there had been the bright and shining possibility, then had come the crushing darkness. Something flickered in his memory. 'Song birds,' he whispered. 'Song birds, yes . . . are taught to sing in the dark.'

That was a line from Oswald Chambers, from one of the books he'd kept by his bed for years. But he couldn't bear switching on the lamp to read it; his eyes had been feeling weak and even painful. He turned on his side and opened the drawer of the nightstand and took out the flashlight. Then he shone the flashlight on the open book.

He thumbed through the familiar pages. There! Page forty-five, the reading for February fourteenth. . . .

At times God puts us through the discipline of darkness to teach us to heed Him. Song birds are taught to sing in the dark, and we are put into the shadow of God's hand until we learn to hear Him. . . . Watch where God puts you into darkness, and when you are there keep your mouth shut. Are you in the dark just now in your circumstances, or in your life with God? Then remain quiet. . . . When you are in the dark, listen, and God will give you a very precious message for someone else when you get into the light.

The flashlight slid onto the bed beside him as he fell asleep, but his hand resolutely gripped the book until dawn.

—Chapter 11
To Sing in the Dark

One of my favorite characters has shown up at Father Tim's table at mealtime.

As he served two plates and got out the flatware, he eyed the old man. Something was wrong. 'Uncle Billy, you're not your old self. I'm going to ask a blessing on our supper, then I'd like you to tell me what's what.'

Uncle Billy clasped his hands under his chin and bowed his head. His left hand was doing its best to keep his right hand from trembling.

'Father, thank You for sending this dear friend to our table, it's an honor to have his company. Lord, we ask You for Bill Watson's strength: strength of spirit, strength of mind, strength of purpose, strength of body. May You shower him with Your mighty, yet tender grace, and give him hope and health all the days of his long and obedient life. We pray You'd heap yet another blessing on Puny for preparing what You've faithfully provided, and ask, also, that You make us ever mindful of the needs of others. In Jesus' name, Amen.'

'A-men!'

—Chapter 14
Waiting for Wings

Could he do it? Could he preach in his old pulpit at Lord's Chapel and bring something worthwhile to the people? He felt jittery about it, unnerved. He needed someone to preach *him* a sermon.

"*'I can do all things through Christ who strengthens me!'*" he shouted aloud from Philippians 4:13.

'Is that merely a few things, Timothy, or is it actually all things?' He walked to and fro in the light-filled study.

'*All* things!' he thundered in his pulpit voice.

There. That should do it.

—Chapter 15
In This Mountain

At two o'clock in the morning, he realized he'd fallen asleep in his chair in the study, and found his notebook on the floor. He regretted waking. There seemed a film over the lamplit room, as if he were wearing sunglasses. It had nothing to do with his eyes and everything to do with his spirit. He felt at the end of himself.

Perhaps he should have gone forward with the medication for depression. The film, the darkness seemed always hovering nearby; if it disappeared for a time, it came back. He felt again a moment of panic—what if he were succumbing, as his father did, to the thing that brought down his marriage, brought down his business, ruined his health?

But he mustn't dwell on that. He must dwell on Sunday's message, for the message still hadn't come right.

He'd be forced to drum up something from days of yore, some antiquity that might be dredged from sermon notes stored in the study cabinet.

But he didn't have what it would take to dredge.

'Lord,' he said, 'speak to me, please. I can't go on like this. Speak to me in a way I can understand clearly. I've read Your word, I've sought Your counsel, I've whined, I've groveled, I've despaired, I've waited. And through it all, You've been silent.'

He sat for a time, in a kind of misery he couldn't define; wordless, trying to listen, his mind drifting. Then at last he drew a breath and sat up straighter, determined.

'I will not let You go until You bless me!' he said, startled by his voice in the silent room.

He took his Bible from beside his chair and opened it at random.

Stop seeking what you want to hear, Timothy, and listen to what I have to tell you.

He felt no supernatural jolt; it happened simply. God had just spoken to his heart with great tenderness, as He'd done only a few times before in his life.

'Yes,' he said. 'Thank you. Thank you.'

Where the book had fallen open in his lap, he began to read, and found the passage only moments later.

The peace flowed in like a river.

Though he'd known for decades the exhortation in First Thessalonians, and had even preached on it a time or two, it came to him now as if it were new, not ancient, wisdom. It came to him with the utterly effulgent certainty that this Scripture was his, and he might seize upon it as upon a bright sword that would pierce . . .

. . . pierce what?

The darkness.

'Thank You,' he whispered, 'for the time of darkness.'

—Chapter 19
A Day in Thy Courts

'I wrestled with this morning's message as Jacob wrestled with the angel, until at last I said to God, "I will not let You go until You bless me."

'I had prayed and labored over a sermon, the title of which is listed in your bulletin and which no longer has anything to do with what I have to say to you this morning.

'What I'd hoped to say was something we all need to know and ponder in our lives, but the message would not convey a deeper truth.

'The reason it would not is simple:

'I was writing the wrong sermon.

'Then, at the final hour, God blessed me with a completely different message—a sermon expressly for this service, this day, this people.'

Father Tim smiled. 'The trouble is, he gave me only four words.

'I was reminded of Winston Churchill, how he was called to deliver the convocation address at his old school. Though this account is likely apocryphal, I believe Churchill would agree with the wisdom of it.

'As he stood to the podium, there was an enormous swell of excitement among the pupils and faculty that here was a great man of history, a great man of letters and discourse, about to tell them how to go forward in their lives.

'Churchill leaned over the podium, looked his audience in the eye, and here, according to legend is the entire text of his address:

'"Young men, never, never, never give up."

'Then he sat down. In truth, saying more may not have had the power to penetrate so deeply, nor counsel so wisely.

'Last night, God gave me four words that St. Paul wrote in his second letter to the church at Thessalonica. Four words that can help us enter into obedience, trust, and closer communion with God Himself, made known through Jesus Christ.

'Here are the four words. I pray you will inscribe them on your heart.'

Hope Winchester sat forward in the pew.

'*In everything . . . give thanks.*'

Father Tim paused and looked at those gathered before him. At Emma Newland . . . Gene Bolick . . . Dooley Barlowe . . . Pauline Leeper . . . Hope Winchester . . . Hélène Pringle. Around the nave his eyes gazed, drawing the congregants close.

'In *everything*, give thanks. That's all. That's this morning's message.

'Generally, Christians understand that giving thanks is good and right.

'Though we don't do it often enough, it's easy to have a grateful heart for food and shelter, love and hope, health and peace. But what about the hard stuff, the stuff that wounds you to the quick? Just what is this *everything* business?

'It's the hook. It's the key. *Everything* is the word on which this whole powerful command stands and has its being.

'Please don't misunderstand; the word *thanks* is crucial. But the deeper spiritual truth lies in giving thanks in . . . everything.

'In loss of all kinds. In illness. In depression. In grief. In failure. And, of course, in health and peace, success and happiness. In everything.

'There'll be times when you wonder how you can possibly thank Him for something that turns your life upside down; certainly there will be such times. Let us, then, at times like these, give thanks *on faith alone* . . . obedient, trusting, hoping, believing.

'Perhaps you remember the young boy who was kidnapped and beaten and thrown into prison, yet rose up as Joseph the King, ruler of nations, able to say to his brothers, with a spirit of forgiveness, "You thought evil against me, but God meant it for good, that many lives might be spared." Better still, remember our Lord and Savior, who suffered agonies we can't begin to imagine, fulfilling God's will that you and I might have everlasting life.

'Some of us have been in trying circumstances these last months. Unsettling. Unremitting. Even, we sometimes think, unbearable. Dear God, we pray, stop this! Fix that! Bless us—and step on it.

'I admit to you that although I often thank God for my blessings, even the smallest, I haven't thanked Him for my afflictions.

'I know the fifth chapter of First Thessalonians pretty well, yet it just hadn't occurred to me to actually take Him up on this notion. I've been too busy begging Him to lead me out of the valley and onto the mountaintop. After all, I have work to do. I have things to accomplish . . . alas, I am the White Rabbit rushing down the hole like the rest of the common horde.

'I want to tell you that I started thanking Him last night—this morning at two o'clock, to be precise—for something that grieves me deeply. And I'm committed to continue thanking Him in this hard thing, no matter how desperate it might become, and I'm going to begin looking for the good in it. Whether God caused it or permitted it, we can rest assured—there is great good in it.

'Why have I decided to take these four words as a personal commission? Here's the entire eighteenth verse:

'"*In everything, give thanks . . . for this is the will of God in Christ Jesus concerning you.*"

'His will concerning you. His will concerning me.

'This thing which I've taken as a commission intrigues me. I want to see where it goes, where it leads. I pray you'll be called to do the same. And please, tell me where it leads you. Let me hear what happens when you respond to what I believe is a challenging, though deceptively simple, command of God.

'Our obedience will say, "Father, I don't know why You're causing or allowing this hard thing to happen, but I'm going to give thanks in it because You ask me to. I'm going to trust You to have a purpose for it that I can't know and may never know. Bottom line, You're God—and that's good enough for me."

'What if you had to allow one of your teenagers to experience a hard thing, and she said, "Mom, I don't really understand why you're letting this happen, but you're my mom and I trust you and that's good enough for me"?'

He looked around the congregation. 'Ah, well,' he said, 'probably not the best example.'

Laughter.

'But you get the idea.

'There are many more words in the first letter to Thessalonica that beg our attention.

'"*Pray without ceasing.*"

'"*Quench not the Spirit.*"

'But the words which God chose for this day, this service, this pastor, and this people, were just these four. "*In everything, give thanks.*"

'Mark these.'

Hélène Pringle realized she had been holding her breath for what seemed a very long time.

'When we go out into the churchyard this morning, let those who will, follow yet another loving command from Paul's letter. "Greet the brethren with an holy kiss!"'

'Amen.'

Miss Pringle exhaled; and then, with the congregation, gave the response.

'*Amen!*'

—Chapter 19
A Day in Thy Courts

Edith Mallory promised Father Tim $25,000 for the Children's Hospital if he would conduct a private service for her. She has preyed upon Father Tim for years. But he never expected anything like this.

He stood dumbstruck, praying the prayer that never fails. What did God want of him in this thing? What could He possibly have intended by bringing him face-to-face with Edith Mallory in a locked room? It was a nightmare.

His knees began to shake. He sat at once in the armchair next to the sofa.

'I'll give you your hour, Edith. Happily. There's a little girl at the hospital right now, four years old—her leg was broken by her uncle because she tried to run from his abuse. Another child was born with a hole in his heart and is facing his third medical procedure. I could go on. The point is, if such an hour as this can spare these children even a moment of suffering . . .'

'You disgust me, Timothy, with your preacher talk. Will you never *weary* of such pap?'

'Never.'

'You're not alone, you know, in wanting to serve God. I want to serve God, too.'

'Yes, of course, but only in an advisory capacity.'

She furrowed her brow.

'You're rude. You were always rude to me, Timothy. I find no excuse for it. Nor would God.' She pouted again, drawing her mouth down at the corners.

He stood. 'Let us begin.' His knees trembled, still. 'Blessed be God; Father, Son, and Holy Spirit.'

He waited for her response. 'Will you respond?'

'And blessed be His kingdom,' she said, snappish, 'now and forever. Amen.'

'Almighty God, to You all hearts are open, all desires known, and from you no secrets are hid . . .' He didn't know how he could get through this; it was a travesty. He sat again.

'Give me a moment,' he said. The message of the morning service, which seemed days in the past, suddenly came to him with the complete conviction with which he'd preached it. *In everything* . . .

'Oh, forget that stuff you learned from a book! I never wanted you to do a full liturgy, anyway, I could never remember all those tiresome responses. All I wanted is for you to talk to me, Timothy, to . . . to hold me.'

She leaned toward him. 'You're a human being, you have feeling and passion like everyone else. Are you so frightened of your passion, Timothy?'

As she placed her hand on his knee, he recoiled visibly, but didn't get up and move away.

Be with me, Lord, forsake me not. I'm going to fly into the face of this thing.

He removed her hand from his knee and took it in his. He was trembling inside, but his hand was steady.

'Let's begin by doing what you asked. Let me pray for you, Edith.' Her hand felt small and cold in his, like the claw of a bird, the palm surprisingly calloused. She flinched, but didn't withdraw her hand— the beating of her pulse throbbed against his own.

He bowed his head. 'Father.'

But he could do no more than call His name. 'Abba!' he whispered. *Help me!*

Christ went up into the mountain; He opened His mouth and taught them . . . *But I say unto you, Love your enemies, bless them that curse you, do good to them that hate you, and pray for them which despitefully use you. . . .*

'Bless your child Edith with the reality of your Presence,' he prayed.

He was forcing himself to intercede for her; it was stop and start, like a mule pulling a sled through deep mire. He quit striving, then, and gave himself up; he could not haul the weight of this thing alone.

'By the power of Your Holy Spirit, so move in her heart and her life that she cannot ignore or turn away from Your love for her. Go, Lord, into that black night where no candle burns, where no solace can be found, and kindle Your love in Edith Mallory in a mighty and victorious way.

'Pour out Your love upon her, Lord, love that no human being can or will ever be able to give, pour it out upon her with such tenderness that she cannot turn away, with such mercy that she cannot deny Your grace.

'Fill her heart with certainty—with the confidence and certainty that You made Edith Mallory for Yourself, that You might take delight in her life . . . and in her service. Yes, thank You, Lord, for the countless thousands she's poured into the work of Your kingdom, for whatever reasons she may have had.' Right or wrong, a good deal of Edith Mallory's money had counted for good over the years, and he would not be her judge.

He was gripping her hand now; he was holding on to her as if she might be taken from him by force.

'Thank you, Father, for this extraordinary time in Your presence, for holding us captive in the circle of Your love and Your grace. With all my heart, I petition You for the soul of this woman, that she might be called to repent and become Your child for all eternity.'

Beads of sweat had broken out on his forehead, though the room was cool.

'Through Christ our Lord,' he whispered. 'Amen.'

He raised his head slowly, feeling an enormous relief.

—Chapter 20
In Everything

And then there's the cry for rain, from *The Book of Common Prayer,* with which we hope to water our gardens and crops.

'O God, heavenly Father, who by Thy Son Jesus Christ has promised to all those who seek Thy kingdom and its righteousness all things necessary to sustain their life: Send us, we entreat thee, in this time of need, such moderate rain and showers, that we may receive the fruits of the earth, to our comfort and to Thy honor; through Jesus Christ our Lord.'

'Amen!'

—Chapter 22
Even to the Dust

There is nothing that makes us love someone so much as praying for them.

—William Law

SHEPHERDS ABIDING

This story of Advent and Christmas is inarguably a reader favorite in the Mitford series. For many, reading it each year has become a family tradition. One reason for its popularity is that we see another facet of Father Tim. As a person who has lived primarily 'in his head,' now he must work with his hands to do what seems impossible. Most important, it must all be done in secret. Not easy in a small town.

After stopping by and visiting Andrew Gregory at the Oxford Antique Shop, Father Tim's imagination is sparked by a discovery.

'Careful where you step,' said Andrew. 'I'm just unpacking a crèche I found in Stow-on-the-Wold; a bit on the derelict side. Some really odious painting of the figures and some knocking about of the plaster here and there . . .'

Father Tim peered at the motley assortment of sheep spilling from a box, an angel with a mere stub for a wing, an orange camel, and, lying in a manger of bubble wrap, a lorn Babe . . .

'Twenty-odd pieces, all in plaster, and possibly French. Someone assembled the scene from at least two, maybe three different crèches.'

'Aha.'

'Not the sort of thing I'd usually ship across the Pond, yet it spoke to me somehow.'

'Yes, well . . . it has a certain charm.'

The day after his visit to Oxford Antiques, he realized that the angel had seized his imagination.

He was surprised by the vivid recollection of her face, which he'd found beautiful, and the piety of her folded hands and downcast eyes.

As for the missing wing, wasn't that a pretty accurate representation of most of the human horde, himself included?

The image of the Babe also came to mind. The craziness and commerce of Christmas, so utterly removed from the verity of its meaning, had served to make the bubble-wrapped figure a profoundly fitting metaphor.

He had every reason in the world not to do it.

First, he'd never attempted anything like this. Not even remotely like this.

Second, it was the sort of project Cynthia might take on and accomplish with great success, but as for himself, he had no such talent or skill.

Third, there would hardly be enough hours left in the year to get the job done, though when he made an inquiry by phone, Andrew offered to help him every step of the way, vowing to call upon his professional resources for advice.

Fourth, the thing was too large, too out of proportion for the corner of the study: some figures were easily fifteen or sixteen inches tall.

Last, but definitely not least, he had enough to do. Nonetheless . . .

Andrew Gregory was polishing a Jacobean chest when Father Tim arrived at Oxford.

He went directly to Andrew and, without formal greeting or further deliberation, said, 'I'll take it.'

He thought his voice quavered a bit when he said this, as well it might.

—Chapters 1 and 2

Hope Winchester secretly plans to purchase Happy Endings bookstore, and asks Father Tim to pray for her.

He peered at his bookseller, smiling. 'I must say, you're looking angelic. Perhaps radiant would be the word.'

She flushed. 'Thank you, Father. I have a secret.'

'Aha.'

'But I can't tell you what it is.'

'Of course you can't, because then it wouldn't be a secret.'

'I need you to pray.'

'Consider it done.'

'God has just given me the most wonderful idea.'

'He does that sort of thing.'

'But it's frightening. And then it's so exciting that I can hardly sleep. It seems such a huge thing, and I've never done a huge thing before.' She took a deep breath. 'I've always done small things.'

'I understand.'

'You do?'

'Oh, yes.'

'Would you ask God to give me wisdom? Would you ask him to . . . guide and direct me in this?'

'I must say, for a brand-new believer, you have a clear understanding of what to ask for. And, yes, I will pray.'

'I don't know if I can do it,' she said, looking anxious. 'All I know is that I want to do it . . . very much.'

'Don't worry about anything, Hope, but in everything, by prayer and supplication, with thanksgiving, make your requests known unto God, and the peace that passes all understanding will fill your heart and mind through Christ.'

'Brilliant,' she said. 'Thank you!'

'Not my words. St. Paul's. Philippians four, verses six and seven.'

'Four, six and seven,' she repeated. 'I'll remember.'

—Chapter 3

'Here we are. . . .'

Andrew was thumbing through a book he'd found at home. 'Look at this, *Vierge et enfant*, it's called . . . the Virgin Mother's robe is black. Foreshadowing the cross, perhaps.'

'No,' said Father Tim. 'No black.' He held the angel carefully, glazing the wing with light, rapid brushstrokes. Before it dried, he'd use his little finger to insinuate the separation of feathers.

Fred ducked through the door. 'I brought th' walnut chest from th' warehouse. You want it in th' window?' he asked Andrew.

'Where the bookcase was sitting. I'll give you a hand after lunch.'

'And I'm off to the Grill,' said Father Tim.

It was the way he stood up, he remembered afterward—the way his leg had somehow twisted, causing him to lose his balance.

As he grabbed for the sink with his left hand, he saw the angel tumble from his right; it seemed to take a very long time to fall. He heard a terrible sound escape his throat, something between a shout and a moan, as the figure crashed onto the slate floor.

The angel was shattered. He was shattered.

There was a long silence in which he and Andrew and Fred stood frozen, unmoving. He realized that his mouth was still open, forming the shout he'd heard himself make.

'Good Lord,' Andrew said at last.

He wanted to burst into tears, but steeled himself. 'What a bumbling fool . . .'

'Please.' He felt Andrew's hand on his shoulder. 'No recriminations. The head is intact, and the wing isn't so bad. What do you think, Fred? Can it be fixed?'

'I think it would take . . . '—Fred cleared his throat—'a mighty long time. Th' body's in a lot of little pieces.'

Father Tim stooped and picked up the head, and was somehow deeply moved to see the face still so serene, and so perfectly, perfectly satisfied.

The adrenaline that pumped in him these last weeks had crashed with the angel. He felt confused, and suddenly old.

—Chapter 6

⁂

Father Tim returns to his work after dropping the angel.

He walked south with Barnabas to the Oxford, where, in the glow of the streetlamp, he unlocked the door and stepped inside.

> '. . . *unto us a child is born,*
> *Unto us a Son is given,*
> *God himself comes down from heaven.*
> *Sing O sing, this blessed morn.'*

Someone had left the CD player on. He went to the cabinet to turn it off, but chose instead the glad company of music.

Though he seldom made a visitation at night, he felt oddly at home in this dark and wax-scented room, secure against the vagaries of the world where wars and rumors of wars perpetually threatened, and hardly anything seemed dependable.

His work, however, was practically calling his name. With Barnabas at his heels, he quickened his step to the back room, eager to see what he and Fred and Andrew had accomplished, and how far they'd come.

Though what he was doing had no deep or earth-shaking significance, God seemed to care that he didn't blow it; He seemed to be guiding his hands, his instincts, his concentration.

Sometimes he and Fred would work for an hour or more without uttering a word, so deep was the absorption. When he regained consciousness, as it were, he often felt he'd been somewhere else entirely, and entirely at peace.

Perhaps this was the benediction of working with one's hands instead of one's head. Indeed, he had hotly pursued the life of the mind nearly all his life. His mother had ardently believed in a healthy balance of physical, mental, and spiritual activity, but as he'd gone away to school and entered into the fray of the world, the balance had slipped, and activity of the mind and spirit had triumphed. His hands, except for gardening, cooking, and washing a dog the size of a double-wide, had engaged in little more than turning the pages of a book.

And look what he'd missed! The figures in a row on the shelf were a marvel to him. Though he was hastening to get it all finished, he would be sorry to see it all end.

He'd completely released the anxiety that his artistic wife would find the work amateurish or heavy-handed. It *was* amateurish! It *was* heavy-handed! But, by heaven, it was also something else, though he couldn't say what.

He shucked off his warm jacket and gloves and picked up a brush and studied it carefully, wondering if he should choose a larger size, which would cover the surface faster.

But, no. He didn't want the Holy Family to go faster. He'd developed a special tenderness toward the last of this worshipful assembly, and wanted to give them his deepest concentration.

Indeed, it seemed to be the wont of most people in a distracted and frantic world to blast through an experience without savoring it or, later, reflecting upon it.

Working on the figures had slowed him down, forced him to pay attention and to savor the work of his hands. This also reminded him daily that Christmas hadn't begun the weekend after Halloween, as the shops in Wesley and even Mitford would have one think. The time of preparation was yet under way—the darkness before the light was still with the world.

His heart lifted up as he dipped his brush into the glaze that would deepen the hues in Joseph's robe.

'Lord,' he said aloud, 'thank You for being with me in this.'

—Chapter 7

He was assailed by the anxiety of moving ahead on his homily for the midnight service at Lord's Chapel, then rummaging through the basement for the Christmas-tree stand and calling The Local about the chocolates and ringing Hope to make sure she had everything on the book list and checking with the Woolen Shop about Sammy's sweater. . . .

Blast it! *No!* He would not forfeit the glad rewards of this rare, unhurried moment. He would not allow the stresses of Christmas to assault him.

He took a deep breath, exhaled, and closed his eyes.

Thank you, Lord, for the grace of an untroubled spirit, and for the blessings which are ours in numbers too great to count or even recognize . . . .

—Chapter 7

'Fred,' said Father Tim, 'have you ever cut hair?'

'I cut my wife's hair once.'

Once. Didn't sound encouraging.

'Turned out she looked s' much like her brother, they thought he'd gone t' wearin' a skirt.'

'Umm.'

'I was in th' doghouse for a good while. But you take my gran'daddy, he was a barber an' a half. Used to barber th' men at shearin' time. Barbered th' neighbors, too, had a good little business set up on th' back porch.'

'I see.'

'Ever' now an' again, he pulled teeth on th' side.'

'Enterprising!'

'Is it you that's wantin' a haircut?'

'It is, Fred, it is.' He heaved a sigh.

'I wouldn't have said anything . . .' Fred left his sentence unfinished, but raised an eyebrow.

Time was flying; it was fish or cut bait. 'What do you need to do the job?'

'Scissors an' a comb.'

'I've got a comb,' said Father Tim.

'I've got scissors,' said Fred.

'While you're at it, I've been having a little trouble with my left molar.'

They laughed. If worse came to worst, he could wear a hat when he left the house, and, as for the Christmas Eve service, it would be pretty dark in the candlelit nave, anyhow.

'Hop on your stool,' said Fred, 'an' I'll be right back.'

He did as he was told. *Lord,* he prayed, *I'd appreciate it if You'd be in on this.*

—Chapter 8

·⸝⸝⸝⸝ ❧ ⸝⸝⸝⸝·

The Mitford gas station owner, Lew Boyd, has secretly married a woman in Tennessee. It's complicated, as you can imagine, and Lew has come to think so, too. He confides the quandary to Father Tim.

'But th' deal's done—she lives with 'er mama an' can't even tell 'er she's married. I ain't told nobody but you, 'cause if I did, th' news would run up th' road quick as a scalded dog.'

'That's true.'

'An', see, I feel like it ain't right of me to expect anything but what we agreed on before we was married.'

'Were you willing to wait then?'

'I was then, but mostly I ain't now.'

'Did you marry her because you love her or because you were a lonely widower?'

'I ain't goin' t' lie. It was some of both. But mostly because I love 'er. She's a fine woman, an' that's a fact.'

'Have you talked to God about this?'

'I go t' church now an' again, but I ain't whole hog on religion.'

'Why is that?'

Lew shrugged. 'Seems like he wouldn't want t' mess with me.'

'Why wouldn't He?'

'I don't know. I've done a good bit of wrong in my life.'

'So have I.'

'Not you!'

'Yes, me.'

'I'll be dogged.'

'It doesn't matter a whit that I'm a priest. What matters is that we surrender our hearts to God and receive His forgiveness, and come into personal relationship with His Son.'

'Earlene, she's got that kind of thing with, you know . . .' He pointed up.

'Would you like to have it?'

Lew gazed out the driver's window, then turned and looked at Father Tim. Tears streamed down his roughly shaven face. 'I don't know, I guess I ain't ready t' do nothin' like that.'

'When you are, there's a simple prayer that will usher you into His presence and change your life for all time—if you pray it with a true heart.'

Lew wiped his eyes on his jacket sleeve.

'How simple is it?'

'This simple: Dear God, thank You for loving me and for sending Your Son to die for my sins. I sincerely repent of my sins and receive Christ as my personal Savior. Now, as Your child, I turn my entire life over to You.'

'That's it?'

'That's it.'

'I don't know about turnin' my entire life over.'

'An entire life is a pretty hard thing to manage alone.'

'Yessir.'

There was a thoughtful silence as the heater blasted full throttle.

'Meanwhile,' said Father Tim, 'why don't we pray about what you've just told me?'

'Yessir. I 'preciate it.' Lew bowed his head.

'Lord, thank You for Your mercy and grace. You know the circumstances, and You've heard Lew's heart on this hard thing.

'All we ask, Father, is that Your will be done.

'In the mighty name of Jesus, Your Son and our Savior, amen.'

'Beggin' your pardon, Father, but that don't seem like much t' ask.'

'It's the prayer that never fails, Lew.'

'Never fails?'

'Never. I hope you'll pray it in the days and weeks to come.'

Lew considered this. 'Exactly what was it again?'

'Thy will be done.'

Lew nodded, thoughtful. 'OK. All right. I can do that. I don't see as there's anything to lose.'

'Nothing to lose, everything to gain.' He clapped Lew on the shoulder. 'You have my word.'

—Chapter 8

As calm as he'd meant to be, as poised as he'd planned to be, he was seeing his good intentions dashed. Christmas Eve had arrived, and there was no rest for the wicked.

Paint, paint, and more paint—he had labored over that camel to beat the band, and so had Fred, and still it was a camel he wouldn't personally want to ride across the desert.

'Lord,' he whispered into the dark room, 'would You please handle everything that comes today? And, as Shakespeare said, "thanks, and thanks, and ever thanks"!'

—Chapter 9

Father Tim is no fan of hurrying the Christmas season, as you can see.

Families would come together from near and far, to savor this holy hour. And afterward, they would exclaim the glad greeting that, in earlier times, was never spoken until Advent ended and Christmas morning had at last arrived.

Call him a stick-in-the-mud, a dinosaur, a fusty throwback, but indeed, jumping into the fray the day after Halloween was akin to hitting, and holding, high C for a couple of months, while a bit of patience saved Christmas for Christmas and kept the holy days fresh.

He knelt and closed his eyes, inexpressibly thankful for quietude, and found his heart moved toward Dooley and Pooh, Jessie and Sammy . . . indeed, toward all families who would be drawn together during this time.

'Almighty God, our heavenly Father . . .' He prayed aloud the words he had learned as a young curate. '. . . who settest the solitary in families: We commend to thy continual care the homes in which thy people dwell. Put far from them, we beseech thee, every root of bitterness, the desire of vainglory, and the pride of life. Fill them with faith, virtue, knowledge, temperance, patience, godliness. Knit together in constant affection those who, in holy wedlock, have been made one flesh. Turn the hearts of the parents to the children, and the hearts of the children to the parents; and so enkindle fervent charity among us all, that we may evermore be kindly affectioned one to another; through Jesus Christ our Lord.'*

In the deep and expectant silence, he heard only the sound of his own breathing.

'Amen,' he whispered.

—Chapter 9

---

* *The Book of Common Prayer*

I know the plans I have for you, says the Lord. Plans for good and not for evil, to give you a future and a hope.

—Jeremiah 29:11

LIGHT FROM HEAVEN

Father Tim and Cynthia are house-sitting at Meadowgate Farm when he is charged with the revival of a mountain church that's been closed for forty years. Dooley is studying to be a veterinarian, and his young brother, Sammy, has been folded into the security of the Kavanagh family. All looks settled until he drives up the road, crosses a creek, and ascends the mountain to Holy Trinity, where a whole other world awaits his affections.

As might be expected, some said that he'd 'saved' Dooley's life. The truth was, Dooley more likely saved his. At the age of sixtysomething, he had gone from an inward-looking bachelor to an outward-striving father. And then, of course, Cynthia had moved in next door. A double miracle if ever there was one.

Lord, he prayed, *thank You for Your continued grace. Help me fulfill Your plan for my life; give me a heart to hear Your voice. . . . And please, if You would do the same for Dooley . . .*

He rolled toward his wife, slipped his arm around her, and felt the deep, drowning mystery of sleep come upon him.

—Chapter 2
The Vicar

'Remember, sweetheart, what James Hudson Taylor said; you've quoted it to me as I plunged into many a Violet book. "There are three stages in the work of God: impossible, difficult, done."'

Cynthia took his hand in hers, and he had at once the consoling knowledge that her touch was a lifeline, thrown out to him by God as directly as if He were present in the room—which, of course, He was.

—Chapter 3
Faithful Remnant

So this is what God had for him.

He turned to the communion rail, and ran his hand along the wood. He rubbed the wood with his thumb, musing and solemn, then dropped to his knees on the bare floor and lowered his head against the rail. Barnabas sat down beside him.

Lord, thank You for preparing me in every way to be all that You desire for this mission, and for making good Your purpose for this call. Show me how to discern the needs here, and how to fulfill them to Your glory and honor.

He continued aloud, 'Bless the memory of all those who have gathered in these pews, and the lives of those who will gather here again.'

Barnabas leaned against the vicar's shoulder.

'I am Thine, O Lord. Show me Thy ways, teach me Thy paths, lead me in Thy truth and teach me.'*

—Chapter 3
Faithful Remnant

He extended his left hand to Cynthia, and his right to Lace. They bowed their heads.

'Lord, we thank You for the great power of Your grace in all our lives. Thank You for Lace and Dooley whom we love and cherish, and for the bright futures You've set before them. Thank You for the gifts You've so generously given Lace, which assisted her in winning this fine scholarship. Thank You for Your gift to Dooley of a heart concerned for all Your creatures, great and small.

'Thank You for Cynthia, who lightens and enriches the spirits of everyone who knows her. And now, Lord, thank You for this bounteous meal of the things Dooley enjoys most, and which we enjoy with him. You are good, O God, and You are faithful. Tenderize and soften our Lenten hearts, we pray, lest they grow brittle and break.

'In the name of our Lord and Savior, Jesus Christ, Amen.'

'Amen!'

—Chapter 4
Agnes

---

* Psalm 25:4

❧

On his first Sunday at Holy Trinity, six people show up to be counted. Hallelujah!

'Brothers and sisters,' he said, as the congregants rose to leave, 'please join Cynthia and me for a simple meal on the stone wall.' The idea had come to him quite out of the blue.

'It's a picnic made for two, but God intended it for eight, which reminds me of the old table grace, "Heavenly Father, bless us and keep us all alive; there's ten of us for dinner and not enough for five!"

'He has given us loaves and fishes this morning, that we might celebrate the beginning of our journey as a congregation, and offer thanks for a marvelous new chapter in the life of Holy Trinity.

'Now, let us go forth to do the work that He has given us to do.'

His small flock responded. 'Thanks be to God!'

Moving along the aisle in his purple Lenten vestments, he sensed in his soul the quickening of Easter.

—Chapter 5
Loaves and Fishes

❧

He ran his fingers over the tooled oak of the pulpit, tracing the path the carving knife had taken.

A crown of thorns. A heart. A dove. A dogwood blossom. And in the center of these, a cross.

'Agnes . . .' That's all he could find to say about the sublime wood carving of her son.

She was proud. 'Yes.'

'Let's thank God!' Indeed, it was pray—or bust wide open.

He took her hands in his, and they bowed their heads.

'We praise You, Lord, we thank You, Lord, we bless You, Lord!

'Thank You for the marvel and mystery of this place, for these thirty remarkable years of devotion, for Your unceasing encouragement to the hearts and spirits of Your servants, Agnes and Clarence, for Your marvelous gifts to Clarence of resourcefulness and creativity, and for Your gift to them both of a mighty perseverance in faith and prayer.

'We thank You for this nave above the clouds in which Your holy name has been, and will continue to be, honored, praised, and glorified. Thank You for going ahead of us as we visit our neighbors, and cutting for each and every one a wide path to Holy Trinity. Draw whom You will to the tenderness of Your unconditional love, the sweetness of Your everlasting mercy, and the balm of Your unbounded forgiveness.

'In the name of the Father and of the Son and of the Holy Spirit.'

'Amen,' they said together.

—Chapter 6
Above the Clouds

·᠊᠊᠊᠊᠊᠊᠊᠊᠊᠊᠊᠊᠊·

Every saint has a past, a sixteenth-century poet had said, *and every sinner has a future.* And all because of what He did for love.

'Christ our Passover is sacrificed for us: therefore let us keep the feast. Not with old leaven neither with the leaven of malice and wickedness; but with the unleavened bread of sincerity and truth . . .'

'As it was in the beginning, is now, and ever shall be, world without end . . .'*

The old words seemed somehow reborn, as his spirit stepped forth to embrace his new parish.

—Chapter 9
Keeping the Feast

'I believe Kenny will find us, or we'll find him,' he told Sammy. 'I'm actually expecting that. But in the end, I have to let it all go to God; it's really His job.'

'He ain't doin' too g-good, if y' ask m-me.'

'Consider this. The Bible tells us that two sparrows once sold for a penny. Yet, one of them shall not fall to the ground without His knowing—and caring. If He cares about a sparrow, I'm inclined to believe He cares about me—and you—even more. How many hairs are on your head?'

Sammy made a face; shrugged.

'God knows how many. Jesus says so, Himself: "The very hairs of your head are all numbered."'

'I ain't believin' 'at.'

'Here's the deal. He made you. He cares about you. He loves you. He wants the best for you.' This was a lot to take in, even, sometimes, for himself.

'And because of all that, He has a plan for you, for your life. That's why we can trust Him to do what's best when we pray the prayer that never fails.'

---

* *The Book of Common Prayer*

'Wh-what prayer is 'at?'

'Thy will be done.'

—Chapter 11
A Clean Heart

Agnes Merton tells Father Tim about her past, confessing that her son, Clarence, was born outside the conventions of marriage.

'During a dark hour in my own life,' he said, 'I learned to recite it from memory, just as you did.'

'Could we say it now?' asked Agnes.

Together, they spoke the words of the psalmist.

> *'Have mercy on me, O God, according to your loving kind-ness;*
> *In your great compassion, blot out my offenses.*
> *Wash me through and through from my wickedness*
> *And cleanse me from my sin.*
> *For I know my transgressions, and my sin is ever before me.*
> *Against you only have I sinned . . .'*

Above the gorge, the clouds began to lift; a shaft of sunlight illumined the ridge.

> *'For behold, you look for truth deep within me,*
> *And will make me understand wisdom secretly.*
> *Purge me from my sin, and I shall be pure;*
> *Wash me, and I shall be clean indeed.*

Make me hear of joy and gladness,
That the body you have broken may rejoice.
Hide your face from my sins
And blot out my iniquities.
Create in me a clean heart, O God.
And renew a right spirit within me . . ."*

—Chapter 11
A Clean Heart

Father Tim returns to Mitford to conduct the funeral of Uncle Billy, a character I will always love.

What if he carried forth this foolish notion and no one laughed? Would that dishonor the man they'd come to honor?

'Psalm fifteen,' he told the graveside gathering, 'says "*the cheerful heart hath a continual feast*." And Proverbs seventeen twenty-two asserts that "*a merry heart doeth good like a medicine*."

'Indeed, one of the translations of that proverb reads "*a cheerful disposition is good for your health; gloom and doom leave you bone-tired*."

'Bill Watson spent his life modeling a better way to live, a healthier way, really, by inviting us to share in a continual feast of laughter. Sadder even than the loss of this old friend is that most of us never really got it, never quite understood the sweet importance of this simple, yet profound ministry in which he persevered.

---

* Psalm 51:1–10

'Indeed, the quality I loved best about our good brother was his faithful perseverance.

'When the tide seemed to turn against loving, he loved anyway. When doing the wrong thing was far easier than doing the right thing, he did the right thing anyway. And when circumstances sought to prevail against laughter, he laughed anyway.

'I'm reminded of how an ardent cook loves us with her cooking or baking, just as Esther Bolick has loved so many with her Orange Marmalade Cakes. In the same way, Uncle Billy loved us with his jokes. And oh, how he *relished* making us laugh, *prayed* to make us laugh! And we did.

'I hope you'll pitch in with me to remember Bill Watson with a few of his favorite jokes. We have wept and we will weep again over the loss of his warm and loyal friendship. But I know he's safe in the arms of our Lord.

'This wondrous truth is something to celebrate. And I invite us to celebrate with laughter. May its glad music waft heavenward, expressing our heartfelt gratitude for the unique and tender gift of William . . . Benfield . . . Watson.'

He nodded to Old Man Mueller, who, only a few years ago, had regularly sat on the Porter lawn with Uncle Billy and watched cars circle the monument.

Old Man Mueller stood, sneezed, and dug a beleaguered handkerchief from his pants pocket.

'Feller went to a doctor and told 'im what all was wrong. So, th' doctor give 'im a whole lot of *ad*vice about how t' git well. In a little bit, th' feller started t' leave an' the doctor says, "Hold on! You ain't paid me f'r my *ad*vice!" Feller says, "That's right, b'cause I ain't goin' t' *take* it!"'

A gentle breeze moved beneath the tent.

I've stepped in it now, thought Father Tim. Not a soul laughed—or for that matter, even smiled.

Mule Skinner stood, nodded to the crowd, took a deep breath, and cleared his throat. This was his favorite Uncle Billy joke, hands down, and he was honored to tell it just like Billy told it—if he could remember it.

'An ol' man and an ol' woman was settin' on th' porch, don't you know.'

Heads nodded. This was one of Uncle Billy's classics.

'The ol' woman said, "You know what I'd like t' have?" Ol' man said, "What's 'at?"'

'She says, "A big ol' bowl of vaniller ice cream with choc'late sauce an' nuts on top!"'

'He says, "By jing, I'll jis' go down t' th' store an' git us some." She says, "You better write that down or you'll fergit it!" He says, "I ain't goin' t' fergit it."'

'Went to th' store, come back a good bit later with a paper sack. Hands it over, she looks in there, sees two ham san'wiches.'

Several people sat slightly forward.

'She lifted th' top off one of them san'wiches, says, "Dadgummit, I told you you'd fergit! I wanted mustard on mine!"'

The whole company roared with laughter.

'That was my favorite Uncle Billy joke!' someone exclaimed.

Coot Hendrick stood for a moment then sat back down. He didn't think he could go through with this. But he didn't want to show disrespect to Uncle Billy's memory.

He stood again, cleared his throat, scratched himself—and went for it.

'A farmer was haulin' manure, don't you know, an' 'is truck broke down in front of a mental institution. One of th' patients, he leaned over th' fence an' said, "What're you goin' t' do with that manure?"

'Farmer said, "I'm goin' t' put it on my strawberries."

'Feller said, "We might be crazy, but we put whipped cream on ours!"'

Bingo! Laughter all around!

On the front row, Lew Boyd slapped his leg, a type of response Uncle Billy always valued.

Thank you, Lord!

—Chapter 13
Flying the Coop

Cleansed somehow in spirit, and feeling an unexpected sense of renewal, those assembled watched the coffin being lowered into place. It was a graveside procedure scarcely seen nowadays, and one that signaled an indisputable finality.

'Unto Almighty God we commend the soul of our brother, William Benfield Watson, and commit his body to the ground; earth to earth, ashes to ashes, dust to dust; in sure and certain hope of the Resurrection unto eternal life, through our Lord Jesus Christ . . .'*

—Chapter 13
Flying the Coop

---

* *The Book of Common Prayer*

-ʒ᠈⤳ ⟩ ᠈⤶ᶻ-

'Hey, son. I'm missing you; just wanted to hear your voice.'

Dooley had never warmed to such outpourings; nonetheless, Father Tim found it best to speak these things. The loss of loved ones always made him reflect.

'I'll be done with finals May tenth, and home on the eleventh.'

'We're praying about your finals; don't worry, you can nail them. You'll never guess what I've been thinking. Remember the time we walked to Mitford School together—it was your first day. You went ahead of me, then thought twice about it and asked me to walk up ahead. You didn't want anybody to think a preacher was following you around.'

Dooley cackled. 'Yeah, well, I got over it.'

At the sound of the laughter he loved, Father Tim's spirit lifted. He would tell him about the money this summer. Maybe they'd trek out to the sheep pasture and sit on the big rock by the pond, or maybe they'd sit in the library—Dooley could have the leather wing chair for this auspicious occasion. Shoot, they might even haul around a few dirt roads in the new truck.

In any case, nearly two million dollars would be an astounding reality to grapple with.

Lord, he prayed, *pick the time and place for this important revelation, and thank You for so constructing his character that he might bear the responsibility with grace . . .*

—Chapter 13
Flying the Coop

·⧽⧽⁂⧼⧼·

'I wish there was something for Sammy,' said Cynthia. 'He'd never stoop to attending Sunday school with a five- and a nine-year-old.'

'Unless . . .' he said.

'Unless?'

'Unless he was your teaching assistant.'

'How do you mean?'

'If there was something he could do with gardening to illustrate your teaching . . . I don't know . . . a seed, growth, the story of new life . . . new life in Jesus . . .'

'I like it,' she said. 'Give me a couple of weeks, let me think it all through.'

He took her warm hand and kissed it. 'Lord, thank You for sending Your daughter into this white field. Thank You for showing her Your perfect way to teach the love, mercy, and grace of Your Son. And help us become children, ourselves, eager to receive Your instruction. Through Christ our Lord . . .'

'Amen.'

'Thank you,' he said to his deacon, aka his wife.

'Thank you back.'

'For what?'

'For being willing to serve at Holy Trinity. It's my favorite of all your churches.'

'Why?'

'Because it's so hungry and imperfect.'

Hungry and imperfect. 'Yes,' he said, laughing. 'Yes!'

—Chapter 14
Hungry and Imperfect

--·›‹›×›‹‹·--

Here he prays for a young mountain girl whose grandmother is in prison for murder and whose mother has an undiagnosed illness.

'May I pray for you, Sissie?'

She bowed her head; he placed his hand upon it.

'Father, I thank You for the marvel of Sissie Gleason. For her bright spirit, her inquisitive mind, her tender heart. Thank You for blessing her life above anything I could ask or think. Prepare a way for her, Lord, that she might become all You made her to be. In Jesus' name . . .'

Sissie squeezed her eyes shut. 'An' Lord, please make Mama better, make Donny quit drinkin', bring Mamaw Ruby home, an' give us cheese dogs f'r supper t'night.'

'Amen!' they said in unison.

He was feeling brighter.

—Chapter 15
Shady Grove

--·›‹›×›‹‹·--

The time has come. In this scene, which has been building in several novels, Dooley receives news from Father Tim that will change everything.

The waiting was over. But where to start? He'd had this conversation a hundred times in his imagination . . .

'How would you like to have your own practice when you finish school?'

Dooley sat down and glanced at his watch. 'Unless somebody gave me a million bucks.'

Dooley eyed him, grinning.

'Don't look at me, buddyroe. I am definitely not your man on that deal. How would you like to have the Meadowgate practice? Hal's retiring in five years, just one year short of when you get your degree.'

'Meadowgate would be, like, a dream. It's perfect, it's everything I could want. But it'll take years to make enough money to . . .'

'What if you had the money to buy it?' Why was he asking these questions? Why couldn't he get on with it? He'd held on to his secret for so long, he was having trouble letting it go.

'Well, yes,' said Dooley, 'but I don't even know what Hal would sell it for. Probably, what do you think, half a million? I've done a little reading on that kind of thing, but . . .' Dooley looked suspicious, even anxious. 'Why are we talking about this?'

'Since he's not planning to include the house and the land, I'd guess way less than half a million. Maybe three hundred thousand for the business and five acres. And if you wanted, Hal could be a consultant. But only if you wanted.'

'Yeah, nice dream.' Dooley checked his watch.

'Let me tell you about a dream Miss Sadie had. It was her dream to see one Dooley Barlowe be all he can be, to be all God made him to be. She believed in you.'

Dooley's scalp pricked; the vicar's heart pounded.

'She left you what will soon be two million dollars.' He had wondered for years how the words would feel in his mouth.

There was a long silence. Dooley appeared to have lost his breath; Father Tim thought the boy might faint.

'Excuse me.' Dooley stood and bolted from the library.

'You don't look so good,' Father Tim said when Dooley returned. 'What happened?'

'I puked.'

'Understandable.'

Dooley thumped into the wing chair, stupefied.

'What do you think?' said Father Tim.

'I can't think. There's no way I can think. You aren't kidding me, are you?'

'I wouldn't kid about these numbers.'

'It makes me sad that I can't thank her. I mean, why did she do it? I was just a scrawny little kid who cleaned her attic and hauled her ashes. Why would she do it?'

'I can't make it any simpler. She believed in you.'

'But why?'

'Maybe because the man she loved had been a boy like you— from the country, trying to make it on his own; smart, very smart, but without any resources whatsoever. It so happens that he made it anyway, as you will, also. But she wanted you to have resources.'

Tears brimmed in Dooley's eyes. 'Man.'

'You want to go out in the yard and holler—or anything?'

'I feel . . .' Dooley turned his gaze away.

'You feel?'

'Like I want to bust out cryin'.'

'You can do that,' he said. 'I'll cry with you.'

—Chapter 19
Bingo

In this service at Holy Trinity, Father Tim helps a man obey the scriptural commandment of confession to the fellowship.

In all his years as a priest, he had experienced few Sundays so dauntingly filled.

'In the fifth chapter of the book of James, we're exhorted to confess our sins, one to another.

'I've always esteemed the idea of confession, and in my calling, one sees a good bit of it. But this notion of confessing our sins *one to another* is quite a different matter. Indeed, it involves something more than priest and supplicant; it means confessing to the community, within the fellowship of saints.

'When I left Holy Trinity on Friday, I was going home. But God pointed my truck in the opposite direction.

'I drove to see someone I've learned to love, as I've learned to love so many of you since coming to Wilson's Ridge.

'We had talked and visited several times, and I could see that his distance from God had made his life uphill both ways. But I always hesitated to ask him one simple question.

'I didn't hesitate this time. I asked him if he would pray a simple prayer with me that would change everything.'

His eyes roved the packed pews, and those seated in folding chairs that lined the aisle. There was Jubal. And all the Millwrights. And Robert and Dovey and Donny, and Ruby Luster holding Sissie on her lap . . .

The thought of having everything changed in our lives is frightening. Even when the things that need changing are hard or brutal, some of us cling to them, anyway, because they're familiar. Indeed, our brother had clung . . . and it wasn't working.

'As part of the service for Holy Baptism, our brother has asked if he might make his confession to all of us here today.

'Before I call him forward, I'd like to recite the simple prayer he prayed, similar to one I prayed myself . . . long after I left seminary.

'It's a prayer you, also, may choose to pray in the silence of your heart. And when you walk again through the parched valley, as you've so often done alone, He will be there to walk through it with you. And that's just the beginning of all that lies in store for those who believe in Him.'

He bowed his head, as did most of the congregation.

'Thank You, God, for loving me. And for sending Your son to die for my sins. I sincerely repent of my sins, and receive Jesus Christ as my personal savior. Now, as Your child, I turn my entire life over to You.

'Amen.'

'Robert Cleveland Pritchard, will you please come forward?'

Robert moved along the crowded aisle, trembling; his knees were water, his veins ice.

'I'd like t' confess t' you . . . ,' he said, 'b'fore God . . . that I didn't do it.'

Father Tim looked out to Miss Martha and Miss Mary, both of whom had forgotten to close their mouths. He saw Lace, riveted by what was taking place; and there was Agnes, pale as a moonflower . . .

'I cain't go into th' details of all th' stuff about m' granpaw, 'cause they's little young 'uns here. But Friday e'enin' I done a thing with Father Tim that I guess I've wanted t' do, but didn't know how t' do. I give it all over t' Jesus, like I should've done when m' buddy talked t' me about it in prison.

'All I can say is, it's good. It's real good.'

—Chapter 20
A Living Fire

Miss Martha had supervised the greening of the church this afternoon. The aroma of pine and cedar filled the nave; sticks of hardwood burned bright in the firebox.

'I wrote a sermon this week,' he said from the pulpit, 'but discovered something as I reflected upon it.

'It told us more than we need to know.'

Someone chuckled. He could have some fun with that, but time was of the essence; a big snow was predicted for tonight.

'Well, Lord, I said, please give me what we do need to know. And He did.

'As many of you are aware, this pulpit was built and beautifully hand carved by one of our own—Clarence Merton. The church was not open when he did it; in fact, there was no earthly assurance that it would ever be open again.

'Yet Clarence chose to build and carve this pulpit, anyway.

'Why would he do that? He did it to the glory of God.

'And then, a vandal broke in, and he took out a knife and began to do his own carving, right on this magnificent pulpit.'

Someone gasped.

'For those of you who haven't seen that particular carving, it's right here.' He leaned to his left and made a gesture toward the oak side-panel.

'I consider it to constitute the most profound sermon that could be preached from this or any pulpit.

'"JC," it reads, "loves CM."'

'When Agnes and Clarence saw what had been done, they might have wept. But what did they do? They gave thanks.

'They might have felt it a sacrilege. But what did they do? They considered it a word from God.

'JC, Jesus Christ . . . loves CM, Clarence Merton.'

A relieved murmur sounded among the congregants.

'The thrilling thing about this inscription is that it's filled with truth, not just for Clarence Merton, but for every one of us on this hallowed eve of His birth.

'In everything God has told us in His Word, He makes one thing very clear:

'He loves us.

'Not merely as a faceless world population, but one by one.

'J.C., Jesus Christ, loves you, Miss Martha. He loves you, Miss Mary. He loves you, Jubal.

'And you and you and you—individually, and by name. "My sheep hear my voice," He says, "and I call them by name."

'On this eve of His birth, some of you may still be asking the age-old question, Why was I born?

'In the book of Revelation, we're told that He made all things—that would include us!—for Himself. Why would He do that? You were made by Him . . . and for Him, for His good pleasure.

'Selah! Think upon that.

'And why was *He* born?

'He came that we might have new life, in Him. What does this gift mean? In the weeks to come, we'll talk about what it means, and how it has the power to refine, strengthen, and transform us, and deliver us out of darkness into light.

'Right now, Clarence has a gift for everyone in this room. And a wonderful gift it is.' He nodded to the crucifer. 'Would you come forward, Clarence?'

Clarence came forward, carrying a large, flat board.

He held it aloft for all to see.

'Oak,' said the vicar. 'White oak, the queen of the forest.

'This is a place for us to carve our own inscription, like the one on the pulpit. The board will be here every Sunday until Easter, and whoever wishes to do it will get help from Clarence, if needed. You don't even have to bring your own tools, we have what's needed. When that's done, we'll hang the board on the wall over there, where years later, others can see it, and be reminded that He loves them, too.'

He gazed a moment at the faces before him, at those whom God had given into his hand.

'*For God so loved the world,*' he said, '*that He gave His only begotten Son, that whosoever . . .*'

Many of the congregants joined their voices with his as they spoke the verse from the Gospel of John.

'*. . . believeth on Him should not perish, but have everlasting life.*

'For this hour,' he said, 'that's all we need to know.'

—Chapter 21
Let the Stable Still Astonish

Preach the gospel at all times. If necessary, use words.

—Popularly attributed to St. Francis of Assisi

HOME TO HOLLY SPRINGS

Home to Holly Springs begins when Father Tim receives a cryptic note, telling him to return to his childhood home in Holly Springs, Mississippi. He travels hundreds of miles and wades through decades of memories, to discover who wrote the note and why.

He squatted between his grandparents' graves and placed a red rose on Nanny Howard's, then turned and placed a yellow rose on his grandpa's mound.

'In the name of the Father and of the Son and of the Holy Spirit,' he said, making the sign of the cross. 'Thank you for loving me. Thank you for the model you set for me, though I was often too blind to see it.'

—Chapter 3

Father Tim comes across some of his mother's belongings, and remembers her and her famous garden.

His mother's old trowel.

When he took it from the box, the worn wooden handle with traces of green paint seemed comfortable in his hand, and oddly consoling. The garden had been her life's work, her confession that something lovely could be wrought from disappointment. Madelaine Kavanagh herself had lived out Rothke's premise that 'deep in their roots, all flowers keep the light.'

During more than one of Holly Springs' famous pilgrimages, hundreds of people had wandered along paths his mother had designed through the woodland grove of four hundred azaleas, and out to the smokehouse with its peony beds and trellises of purple wisteria.

It was prophesied that nobody would travel four miles from town to see a garden, especially in wartime when gas was rationed and car parts were unavailable and the auto mechanics had been shipped out to Europe. But his mother, who longed to share her gardens with one and all, had been of a stubborn and visionary stripe. If she could not live in town, she would bring the town to her.

—Chapter 4

In the end, the only assurance he'd ever been able to offer his mother was his love. He would give anything to feel that had been enough, but it had not been enough.

His hands trembled as he put on the stole and poured wine into the small chalice.

'Timmy?'

'Yes, ma'am?'

There was a long silence, then she said, 'There's someone at the door.'

He knelt and took her cold hand and held it against his cheek.

'They've come to see the gardens,' she whispered. 'Tell them . . .' She tugged at his hand, urgent.

'I'm here, Mother.'

'Tell them . . .'

He knew the sound; in the old days, it had been called the death rattle. He bent closer and listened.

'Tell them . . . I'm so sorry, but . . .'

He clasped her hand in both of his.

'. . . the garden is closed.'

He continued to kneel beside her, frozen in place, looking at the bluish shadow of her eyelids and the nearly invisible veins beneath her cheekbones.

He kissed her forehead. Then he released her hand—it seemed to take a long time to lay it at her side—and, still kneeling, offered the supplication he'd memorized from the 1928 prayer book.

'"Into thy hands, O merciful Saviour, we commend the soul of thy servant, now departed from the body. Acknowledge, we humbly beseech thee, a sheep of thine own fold, a lamb of thine own flock, a sinner of thine own redeeming. Receive her into the arms of thy mercy, into the blessed rest of everlasting peace, and into the glorious company of the saints in light. Amen."'*

He stood up and drew the sheet over her face, and went to the kitchen, where Louis and the doctor and nurse were drinking coffee, and said, 'She's gone.'

Louis uttered a primordial howl that might have been his own if he would allow it.

---

* *The Book of Common Prayer*

The funeral home dispatched a hearse to Whitefield, and afterward, he had gone to his room and stood at the open window for a long time, looking out to the moon-washed garden. He had never felt such agony; it was as if he couldn't possibly go on . . .

—Chapter 6

⁘❧❧⁘

Father Tim visits Peggy Cramer, his fiancée during his seminary years. It was not a happy relationship.

'I hear you're married,' she said. 'I'm so glad.'

He was Pavlov's dog; he pulled out his wallet and leaned across the table to show her his family. With some feeling, she said all the things he never tired of hearing.

He slipped the wallet into his pocket and folded his napkin and placed it on the table.

'Well, then,' he said.

They stood in the foyer for several minutes and talked—of the success of the most recent spring Pilgrimage, of the entrance hall's elaborate French wallpaper mural, of the heat.

'Thank you for apologizing, Peggy; it means a great deal.' He took her hand. 'I apologize to you, as well. When you drove out to the house that day, I acted of my own accord. My actions were heedless, and entirely without regard for you. I'm sorry.'

'We were young,' she said.

'I hope you know that God has forgiven us both.'

Her smile was ironic. 'I do know that God has forgiven me, but I can't seem to forgive myself.'

'That,' he said, 'is the hard part. May I pray for you?'

She gripped his hand. 'Please.'

He took a deep breath. 'Father, thank you for arranging this time together, and for the presence of your Holy Spirit. Thank you in advance for blessing your child, Peggy, with the courage to forgive herself as you have so freely forgiven her. And thank you, Father, for faithfully using the hard things in our lives for great good, and for your loving redemption of our souls for all eternity, through Christ our Lord. Amen.'

They stood together for a moment, silent. 'Thank you,' she said. 'Thank you.'

—Chapter 8

There were always chocolate cookies in a round tin with a picture of Santa Claus on the lid. And his grandpa would always grin really big and wiggle his eyebrows as he dug around in the basket for the tin. 'Ho, Timothy!' he always said when he pulled it out. Then they'd take the lid off and say a blessing and eat the cookies before they ate the other stuff. Always.

This evening before dark, he had helped his grandpa toss hay off the truck bed to his twenty-one steers, then they'd straggled to the house and foraged in the basket and shook the cookie crumbs from the tin into their hands.

His grandfather prayed in a really loud voice. 'Make us ever thankful for crumbs as well as banquets, in the name of our Lord, Jesus Christ!'

'Amen!' they said, and licked the crumbs from their salty palms without washing up first.

—Chapter 10

Father Tim reunites with Peggy Winchester, who helped raise him and disappeared from his childhood without saying goodbye. Now he learns why.

'Peggy.' He took her right hand in both of his; her palm was as smooth as the hide of an acorn. 'Why did you leave without saying goodbye?'

She raised her head and looked at him directly; the lamplight on the red bandanna was a flame in the darkened room.

'I was carrying a child.

'I knew I would have to leave Whitefield. Not a living soul knew th' truth, but your mother guessed. I was straightenin' up th' bed-clothes in th' hall closet when she came an' found me. She was very calm. She said, You're going to have a child.

'I said, Yes, ma'am. I never lied to your mother an' I could not do it then.

'I covered my face with my hands for my shame, my terrible shame, but that was not enough covering. I sat on th' closet floor and pulled a blanket over my head and wept. I wept for her, mostly, mostly for her, an' for you. Your mother sat on the little stool that stayed in th' closet an' kept watch over me. She didn't move, and never said a word.

'I could tell, somehow, that she knew it was your father's child.'

He felt as if he's been injected with a paralyzing drug; he could not move his mouth nor avert his gaze from hers. He stared into her eyes as if looking down a long corridor in which he might wander, lost, for all time. He'd spent seventy years journeying to the pew at Christ Church this morning. Now he'd arrived in this place—not a moment too soon or too late—only to find the shattered pieces falling again.

'The next morning, I left the little house I loved, an' you, who I loved better than anything on earth, an' your mother, the kindest woman I'd ever known. No one knew where I was goin', an' except for your mother, no one knew why I left. I took the clothes on my back an' the Bible your mother gave me at Christmas.

'In all the days of my long life, I never hurt so deep as I hurt then, for the suffering I would bring to people who had been kind an' loving to me.'

She appeared suddenly worn beyond telling, though her gaze was steady. 'I'm sorry to tell you this, so sorry to tell you this.'

He could feel himself running, see himself running.

'Are you sure?' he asked. 'Absolutely sure?'

'Yes, I'm sure.'

'You said only Mother knew why you left.'

'Yes. Your father didn't know.'

What was he to do with what she was telling him? Where was he to go with this? *Lord*, he prayed.

'Why are you telling me this now, Peggy? Why tell me after all these years? Did you have the child? What happened to the child?'

He looked up as Henry came quietly into the room and stood beside Peggy. He had taken off his jacket and rolled up the sleeves of his white shirt; there were dark bruises on his arm.

'Henry is your father's son,' she said.

Henry's face was gray. 'I'm sorry. Truly sorry.'

'Henry didn't want to do this,' said Peggy. 'But it had to be done. I prayed that God would help you find it in your heart to understand.'

She looked at him intently; a weight pressed upon his brain. He was inclined to shake his head and somehow clear it, but he couldn't.

'As a little boy, you often prayed for a brother,' said Peggy. 'God in his wisdom answered your prayer, but in a hard way, I know.'

From somewhere above, he was gazing down on the room—at the top of the red bandanna, at Henry's head and his shoulders sloping beneath it, at his own head with its balding patch—the three of them forming a kind of triangle in the lamplit room. The sense that he had somehow risen beyond himself lasted only a moment, yet it seemed to absorb his attention for a long time.

'Why are you telling me this now?' he asked.

'My son cares for me when I'm ailin', loves me when I'm unlovable, an' made this old place like new—all that an' more. Henry has done everything for me. An' I'm willin' to do anything for Henry.'

'He has a disease that I can't pronounce an' can't spell, but it's slowly killin' him.'

Henry continued to stand, his color ashen.

"For a good while, Henry's been weak as pond water, runnin' fevers, feelin' bad, not himself a'tall. He went up to Memphis in May, to a good doctor. They did tests.'

'What did they find?' he asked Henry.

'Acute myelogenous leukemia. There's a lack of new red blood cells, and the white blood cell and platelet counts are very low.' Henry pushed a rolled-up sleeve above his elbow. 'That's the reason for the bruising. Essentially, my bone marrow isn't producing enough new blood cells.'

'Some of his blood cells have cancer,' said Peggy. 'They're takin' over his healthy cells. Th' outcome of that is, Henry will die . . . if we don't do somethin'.'

Henry looked at his mother, seemingly agonized.

'Henry needs a stem cell transplant.' Peggy was calm, even cool. 'They used to call it a bone marrow transplant, but now they got a new way of doin' it.'

The fan moved the air, the clock ticked. He was in a kind of free fall.

'Best thing is to have a brother or sister donate th' stem cells,' she said. Peggy Lambert Winchester was a locomotive hurtling along the track, not stopping at the stations. She looked at him, her eyes wide, her breath short. 'Sister can't do it, too much heart problems, an' anemic since she was a child.'

'You're sure about the diagnosis?' he asked Henry.

'They drilled into my pelvis and pulled out bone marrow with a syringe. They're sure.'

'What happens if you don't get the transplant?'

'They say I could live for some months. A lot of transfusions and antibiotics. Chemo would help, but not for long.'

'What happens if you do get the transplant?'

'Rejection and infection can be serious problems,' said Henry, 'along with the possibility of liver or kidney failure. And yet, there's the possibility that God would grant me a few more years, that I could live a normal life. Any way you look at it, there's no guarantee of success. But I would take that. I would take it gladly.'

'You want me to donate the stem cells.'

'Yes,' said Peggy. 'We do.' Tears spilled along her cheeks.

'When Mama began praying about this, I was completely against getting in touch with you. I tried to put myself in your shoes, and I knew it was too much to ask. But God and Mama are a force to be reckoned with.

'I guess I never really believed you'd come, and that would be all right. I've lived a full life—I've met a lot of good people, seen beautiful places, and I know where I'm going when I pass.

'Then we heard you were in Holly Springs, and I knew God had answered a selfish prayer. And I admit that, for the first time, I began to hope.

'I don't want to leave Mama at this late stage, though Sister would do all she could to help. But I want you to know that I'm not expecting anything, I have no right to expect anything. It's enough to meet you, Tim, to see you face-to-face. I've heard about you all my life, it was a comfort to know you were out there somewhere. You've always been . . . '—Henry paused, moved—'a brother to me.'

He was overwhelmed to think that he'd been counted as a brother to someone all these years, that God had used such a fragile scrap for binding.

—Chapter 16

❦

The track was hammered smooth as iron, though muddy in places from the late rain. He leaped the puddles and kept moving, his breath short but regular.

The peace was beginning to flow in, if only a little.

Forgive my hard heart toward my dad. Forgive me for convicting him when he was innocent. And please help me love him not less, but all the more in everything I've learned this day.

I've got a lot to download on your mercy and grace. I've always rushed to you and dumped whatever it was and hurried away. I want to turn all this over to you slowly, carefully, examining every fragment as I pass it off, so there'll never be any question about it again. Every time I've dumped and run, I've nearly always run back and snatched it out of your hands. Help me in this, and in any uncertainty that lies ahead.

Right now, I'm absolutely certain of only one thing—that you love us, and that's where we all have to begin.

When he, Timothy, was sixty years old, no dog the size of a sofa had yet come into his life, no thrown-away boy with a galaxy of freckles, no good-looking next-door neighbor with legs that set the Main Street Grill on its head. He had been an old bachelor mired in his books, his armchair, and the fray of his parish. And look what had happened—his whole life had been changed forever.

There was no way in which he deserved to become the husband, indeed the soul mate, of a remarkable woman, and yet God Almighty had set her down in the yellow house across the hedge from the rectory, and there it was—a joy to be chosen or refused. He had almost refused.

And Dooley. When Dooley came to live with him, there had been no thought of refusing, though at the time he was completely clueless about the extraordinary rewards that lay ahead.

In like manner, Henry Winchester's best years might lie before him—if he was given the chance to choose.

There were the cows at rest in the deep shade of trees near the water, looking at him, curious.

He stopped in his tracks and crossed himself.

There were twenty or thirty of them, and no bull as far as he could see. Sunlight filtered through the canopy of trees, casting patterns onto the dark sheen of their hides and the surface of the water. He dropped to his haunches and gazed at them. It was among the loveliest sights he'd ever witnessed.

He leadeth me beside the still waters, he restoreth my soul.

—Chapter 18

He had read in Second Timothy this morning, believing, as he had since a boy, that St. Paul had somehow directed the letter to him as well as to the earlier Timothy.

To Timothy, my dearly beloved son: Grace, mercy, and peace, from God the Father and Christ Jesus our Lord.

After years of delving the contents, he knew the epistle by heart.

For God hath not given us the spirit of fear; but of power, and of love, and of a sound mind.

He realized that each time he went to the letters, he possessed some looming apprehension of one sort or another to which this verse inevitably applied.

—Chapter 20

He is intent, now, on helping to save the life of his brother, who, until this trip back home, he didn't know existed.

As earnestly as he'd yearned for his father to love him, he had wanted to be able to love his father. Perhaps now he could love his father in his brother, Henry—and even in himself. Certainly he could love the man in the hosta grove who had looked at his wife with such unguarded tenderness. He could love the man who paid a dear price to protect a young black boy from harm. He could love the man who had taken his son's hand and walked around the barn on the frozen eve of Christmas.

Feeling the weight of his own exertions, he sat in the chair by the window and dozed until the nurse came in and removed the empty IV bag.

Before the infusion, he'd been allowed to administer the sacraments, which had given them both an ineffable calm. Now that the infusion was complete, the sense of helplessness returned.

'I can only pray,' he said, standing again by Henry's bed.

'But that's enough,' said Henry. 'More than enough.'

'Many people are lifting petitions for God's mercy and grace in the life of Henry Winchester. This prayer simply beseeches God to hear all of us who're praying, and grant answers according to his will.'

He adjusted the mask again, and bowed his head and recited the old prayer he'd esteemed since seminary.

'Almighty God, who has promised to hear the petitions of those who ask in your son's name: we beseech you mercifully to incline your ear to us who have made our prayers and supplications unto you, and grant that those things which we have faithfully asked according to your will, may effectually be obtained to the relief of our necessity, and to the setting forth of your glory.'*

He made the sign of the cross over Henry. 'In the name of the Father and of the Son and of the Holy Spirit.' He pronounced the word as he had done as a child—in the Baptist manner, with the long *a*: 'Amen.'

—Chapter 31

---

* *The Book of Common Prayer*

And the parched ground shall become a pool.

—Isaiah 35:7

IN THE COMPANY OF OTHERS

Father Tim travels with Cynthia to the country of his Irish ancestors, staying with Anna and Liam Conor at a quaint fishing lodge. But their vacation is anything but relaxing—a priceless painting is stolen and they end up in the middle of a family's toxic feud. On the upside, we meet one of my favorite dogs in the series.

Anna Conor shares a painful family secret with Father Tim.

'To Liam's mother, I was but a lowly servant girl, just as she'd been. For Liam to love me was a deep sting to her, and because she couldn't hurt me with her tormenting, she tried to hurt Liam instead. One night when she was very drunk, she told me something that was—in its own way—as . . .'

Her face colored with an old fury. 'She told me Mr. Riley wasn't Liam's father.'

'She confessed to you, then.'

She came and sat at the table. 'I don't know if it's true, there's no way to know. She often said crazy, mindless things.'

'Why do you believe she told you this?'

'I think she believed I would tell Liam in one of the dreadful fights he and I had in those days. But of course I would never tell him such a terrible thing.' Her voice shook with the trembling in her. 'The truth is of no importance in the end, Reverend, because Mr. Riley loved Liam very much. I'm sure he never knew he wasn't Liam's father.

'My hatred for her is so cruel, it devours me even yet. Sometimes I feel my heart would break for Liam—knowing the truth doesn't always set us free, Reverend.

'I confess my weakness of faith, my hurtful selfishness, the sin of this consuming hatred that withers my bones. I want to let it go.' A long keening came out of her. 'I want to let it all go.'

—Chapter 11

After speaking with Anna, Father Tim talks with her husband, Liam. Liam is unsure who his father is and is unwilling to ask his mother for the truth.

It was a foolish question, but so be it. 'Can you talk to your mother?'

Liam laughed. 'You spent an afternoon in her company. You know there's no talkin' to my mother. I've had no peace, none a'tall; th' heaviness of it comes between Anna an' me sharp as any blade. I don't know how to run from th' truth like some people do—it's always there, festerin'.'

'I believe what's needed is forgiveness.'

'I don't follow you.'

'I mean you need to do some forgiving, Liam.'

'For the bloody horror of th' whole mucking business, *I* need to do some forgiving?'

'Starting with your mother.'

'For God's sake, you can't mean that—'t is a bloody Protestant joke.'

'I do mean it. One must begin somewhere, sometime, to let go of the bitterness, or be eaten alive and the marrow sucked out.

'As we forgive, we are in that same instant forgiven. It is a sacred two-for-one, a hallowed tit-for-tat.'

He wanted that for Liam.

—Chapter 20

❦

Father Tim continues to counsel the Conor family, trying to help them forgive and move on from past hurts. Here he speaks with Anna about the estrangement from her daughter, Bella.

'Do whatever you can, Anna, to find common ground, and if you do nothing more, forgive her and pray for her. Whenever she lashes out, whenever she draws away, pray and forgive, forgive and pray.'

'Is it too late?' She wept openly now.

'It's never too late, please believe this. There's a scripture in the book of Joel—*I will restore unto you the days the locusts have eaten.* He's fully able to do it, and waiting for you to ask.'

—Chapter 23

Father Tim talks with Evelyn Conor, Liam's elderly, alcoholic mother.

'Faith is radical and often difficult. It's the narrow footpath, not the broad wagon road. Have you asked him to take the fear away?'

'He should be good enough to do it without being asked. He's God, after all.'

He touched her forehead, prayed for her—for the fear to be released, for peace to flow in.

In the long silence, her even breathing. 'What shall I do without you?' she said.

'You'll do just fine without me. You have the one who's always available—for peace, mercy, grace, forgiveness—you name it. And of course there's Fletcher as long as she's needed, and Seamus and Liam and Anna and Tad and Feeney . . .'

'Anna, perhaps, but not Liam,' she said. 'I was unfair to her, but I've been especially unfair to Liam. How does one know, Reverend, what a mother is supposed to be if one has had no mothering? I suppose mothering comes from a place of deep feeling, but after the fire, that place was locked away.'

'Ask Liam to forgive you.'

'Paddy,' she said, her thoughts elsewhere. 'I tried to help him—with everything—but in all the wrong ways, I see.'

'Ask Paddy to forgive you.'

She gave him a fierce look. 'If I do all you say, Reverend, I shall be a hundred years old before I catch up.'

He laughed. Then laughed some more.

She smiled a little. 'Bloody Protestant,' she said.

—Chapter 40

Father Tim is enjoying Holy Week in Ireland. Here, he and Cynthia visit a holy well.

A warm day, the midges in great number. They found Tobernalt at once serene and celebratory. Visitors were inclined to leave ribbons, beads, trinkets of all sorts hanging from every bush and tree. Coins slept like fish at the bottom of a clear pool, people spoke in whispers or not at all. And all the while, the cool, natural spring burbling up in the heart of the ancient forest as it had done long before St. Patrick arrived as a slave boy.

They prayed for those at home, both here and abroad, for safe travel whenever that might be, and for God's blessing upon the Eire and its people. Though against everything in his nature, not to mention the Scout's oath to leave things better than they were found, he wanted to offer something, too—something beautiful, from the heart, not bought over a counter.

He went through his pockets and found the Connemara Black with its feather from the crest of a golden pheasant, dark fur from a seal, and a beard hackle from a blue jay.

He held it in his hand and Cynthia put on her glasses and looked at it again. 'So delicate and beautiful. Are you sure you want to leave it?'

He couldn't say why, exactly, but he did want to leave it. She sketched it—for posterity, she said—and he hung it on the smallest of twigs and thought it handsome there.

—Chapter 40

Evelyn Conor has called her family together, to confess her supremely selfish and arrogant behavior and to ask their forgiveness. Father Tim is invited to join Evelyn's Catholic priest, Father Tad, at her bedside. This scene promotes one of the great, proverbial truths: It's never too late.

'What may I do?' asked Father Tim.

'Whatever you like—pray, read a Psalm, just be there,' said Tad. 'I'd like to keep it simple, let the spirit move. She's set on making her confession to the whole family—can't say I ever witnessed such an event.'

'She seems entirely ready to be sober, to let God have control.'

'The family is grateful, Tim, as am I. Thanks for everything.'

He grinned. 'I was all they had.'

Carrying a stethoscope, Dr. Feeney entered the room first, then Anna, Bella, Liam, Cynthia, himself, and Tad. They formed a half circle around the bed.

Evelyn's breathing was even, her eyes closed—she might have been sleeping. The early evening light came in to them; he saw a rose in a vase on her table.

Tad made the sign of the cross. 'In the name of the Father, and of the Son, and of the Holy Spirit.' Without opening her eyes, Evelyn signed the cross.

'May God, who has enlightened every heart, help us to know our sins and trust in His mercy. Amen.'

Evelyn opened her eyes, looked around the room.

'I made my last confession to a Roman priest and Almighty God before I was married sixty-five years ago. I confess that immediately afterward, I waged a cruel self-determination against my husband's love of God and Church. Riley Conor was a good man, but I had taught myself to despise what was good.'

Her forefinger tapped the coverlet.

'I confess to you, Liam, my son, that you came into this world a motherless child. I have missed the many years of knowing the kind and curious lad you were and the kind and earnest man you've become.'

Liam broken by this, his hand over his face, Anna's arm around him.

'I confess to you, Anna, that I was jealous of your beauty, your thoughtful ways, and your steadfast love for my son.'

Liam to his knees at the foot of the bed, Anna to hers.

The room and all in it, frozen but for tears—the loosing of regret.

'Father O'Reilly, I confess to charging you never to speak of God to me, and though you never spoke of him, you revealed him in faithful concern for my well-being, and in honoring your promise to my departed husband.

'If God gives me breath, I will do all in my power to right these wrongs, and many which we've no time nor strength to name. And more than anything I would ask this of God—so newly known to me, and yet so long familiar—that I will be forgiven by him and by each of you, for these and other sins of which I truly repent.'

He and Cynthia went to their knees.

'God, the Father of mercies,' said Tad, 'through the death and resurrection of his Son, has reconciled the world to himself and sent the Holy Spirit among us for the forgiveness of sins. Through the ministry of the Church, may God give you pardon and peace.

'Evelyn Aednat McGuiness Conor . . .' Tad made the sign of the cross over the penitent. 'I absolve you from your sins in the name of the Father, and of the Son, and of the Holy Spirit.'

—Chapter 43

The lowest ebb is the turn of the tide.

—Henry Wadsworth Longfellow
*A Continual Feast: Words of Comfort and
Celebration Collected by Father Tim*

SOMEWHERE SAFE WITH SOMEBODY GOOD

In *Somewhere Safe with Somebody Good*, Father Tim still feels adrift after retiring. But when offered a chance to return to the pulpit, he declines the offer. By the way, priests aren't relegated exclusively to the pulpit, as Father Tim soon proves with his new 'flock.' Meanwhile, Lace and Dooley navigate the trials of their long-distance relationship, and Sammy struggles to overcome the wounds of abandonment.

Barnabas can no longer navigate the stairs at night and is sleeping in the study. Father Tim decides to sleep on the study sofa a few nights until Barnabas acclimates.

He sat on the floor next to Barnabas, who had made quick work of his burger and fallen asleep immediately after their walk. He ran his fingers into the bristly coat, searching out the steady rhythm of his good dog's heartbeat, and feeling his own separation anxiety.

'Visit this place, O Lord,' he prayed, 'and drive far from it all snares of the enemy; let your holy angels dwell with us to preserve us in peace; and let your blessing be upon us always; through Jesus Christ our Lord.'*

His dog rolled on his side and looked up—it was that slow, lingering look that spoke volumes could he but read them. He thought the look might be saying, It's okay, it's fine down here; I don't mind, you can stop feeling guilty now.

—Chapters 4 and 6

'To carry forth full confession,' he said, 'I'm also sorry I fell asleep after your great dinner on Tuesday.'

'I consider it a compliment.'

'Falling asleep on our anniversary and not even helping with the dishes. That's a compliment?'

'You feel comfortable with me. I don't think I'm a particularly comfortable person.'

'Thanks for helping keep watch.'

'If you're sleeping down here with Barnabas, I'm sleeping down here with Barnabas. How many nights?'

'One more, I think.' He closed his eyes, spoke aloud their favored prayer from the Compline.

'Before the ending of the day / Creator of the world we pray . . .'

---

* *The Book of Common Prayer*

She joined her voice with his. 'That thou with wonted love shouldst keep . . .

'Thy watch around us while we sleep . . .'

The prayer ended, the fire crackled and sighed.

—Chapter 4

· ﹍❧ ➤ ☙﹍·

The bishop has asked Father Tim to fill in as vicar at Lord's Chapel after the replacement priest, Father Henry Talbot, becomes involved in a scandal.

There was something to be said for the invitation being dropped into their lives like a grenade.

One, it demanded that he concentrate every power on making the right decision.

Two, there was no room to agonize over what to do about Sammy.

Restless beside his wife, who had fallen asleep at once, he sought peace in the familiar. *Lord Jesus, stay with us, for evening is at hand and the day is past; be our companion in the way, kindle our hearts, and awaken hope, that we may know thee as thou art revealed in Scripture and the breaking of bread. Grant this for the sake of thy love, amen.**

For the sake of thy love, he thought. For the sake of thy love.

—Chapter 9

---

* *The Book of Common Prayer*

·⟶⟶✗⟵⟵·

In any decision making, he'd learned to wait for the peace; it was heedless to make a move without it. There was no time for waiting, and yet waiting was imperative.

He remained on his knees, prayed aloud. 'Heavenly Father, in whom we live and move and have our being: We humbly pray thee so to guide and govern us by thy Holy Spirit, that in all the cares and occupations of our life we may not forget thee, but may remember that we are ever walking in thy sight . . .'*

He moved directly then to the abridged version. 'Help me, Jesus.'
—Chapter 9

·⟶⟶✗⟵⟵·

Dooley and Father Tim discover Father Talbot alone in the woods, after the priest attempted suicide by ingesting a cocktail of pharmaceuticals.

This was a dream, nothing about it smacked of reality. He shivered in the damp air and felt around for the jacket to wrap about Henry Talbot, but it was saturated with a cold slime, and useless.

He had spent a few nights camping with youth groups, but was hardly an outdoorsman. The silence unsettled him; he needed the sound of the human voice, he needed something to put under the head of a broken man lying in the woods, surrendered to fear and remorse. There was nothing to do but wait for Dooley to come back with medical help. He hunkered on the ground by Henry's side.

---

* *The Book of Common Prayer*

'"Living darkly, with no ray of light . . ."' He repeated Henry's quote, drawn from the half-delirious poem by John of the Cross.

'"And darker still, for I deserved no ray."' Henry's voice might have emanated from an octave never before heard.

'God loves you, Henry.'

'"Love can perform a wondrous labor . . . and all the good or bad in me takes on a penetrating savor . . ."'

His hand gripped Henry's shoulder, to give some mite of warmth.

'It is very hard to die. Or if I have died, I confess I expected more.' A deep tremor in Henry's body, his whole frame agitated, the breath ragged. 'Perhaps this is purgatory, or I have passed directly to Sheol. But the people . . . the people . . .'

'Tell me.'

'Tell them I learned to love them. Lying here, it came to me that I love them and deeply repent of my cold disfavor toward them and our Lord. I was unable, I was coaching then. Ask them to forgive my manifold sins against God and this parish.'

He placed his hand on Henry's head and prayed aloud. 'Nothing can separate us from your love, O Lord. Thank you for releasing us from the bondage of believing we are worthless and rejected . . .'

'Up there . . .' Henry's voice coarse from the heaving.

The moon had escaped cloud cover and silvered the canopy of branches. 'Up there, the heavenly realm, and here, O Lord, am I, a worm awaiting your claim. Will you have me?'

'He will have you, Henry.'

'"Living darkly, with no ray . . ."'

Their voices mingled on the night air.

'For you, Lord,' he prayed, 'have not given us the spirit of fear, but of power and of love and of a sound mind . . .'

'"... and quickly killing every trace of light,"' Henry whispered, '"I burn myself away."'

—Chapter 13

Hope Winchester, the owner of the local bookstore, has struggled with a dangerous pregnancy. The town rallies around her, praying for her health and that of her unborn child.

'The Body of Our Lord Jesus Christ, which was given for you, Hope, preserve your body and soul unto everlasting life. Take and eat this in remembrance that Christ died for you, and feed on him in your heart by faith, with thanksgiving.'*

'The Blood of our Lord Jesus Christ, which was shed for you, Hope, preserve your body and soul unto everlasting life. Take this in remembrance that Christ's Blood was shed for you, and be thankful.'

She allowed the wine to touch her lips but did not drink. 'Amen,' she said. And there was the warmth, so long gone from her, and some sense, at last, of her own living presence.

'It's embarrassing, all those signs saying "Pray for Hope," and the stir in the newspaper . . .'

'Why is it embarrassing?'

'It seems to ask so much of people. Why should they pray for me when they have tribulations of their own?'

'All the more reason to pray for you—prayer is a healing exercise for us as well as for you. Further, you gave us a bookstore, which should be reason enough. Here's an idea. Why don't we pray for those

---

* *The Book of Common Prayer*

who're praying for you? Sort of a back-atcha that has its own loveli-
ness. What do you think?'

'I would never . . . yes, let's do it, yes.'

'Thank you, Father, for every soul who lifts a petition for Hope,
for Scott, and for this special child you're giving into our lives. Bless
those whom you call to pray for Hope, that they would be comforted
in their own hard circumstances and shielded in their joy. Thank you
for the supernatural connections that prayer creates among us, for
the ties it so strongly binds. In the name of Jesus who is all hope,
Amen.'

—Chapter 15

Lace is home from university and stops by for a visit with Father
Tim, now the manager of Happy Endings bookstore.

'How did you know what you wanted to do with your life?' said Lace.
'I'm constantly trying to figure that out for myself.'

'I'm not sure I figured it out. I was chiefly motivated by the notion of changing my father's heart if I became a priest.'

'Did you change his heart?'

'I don't believe my priesthood ever mattered to him in the way I
hoped it would. God knows. What do you think you want to do with
your life?'

'If . . . Dooley and I get married, I would like to work in the practice with him. But would that be . . . I don't know, enough?'

'How do you mean?'

'I wonder about making a commitment to the practice and then
discovering it isn't enough. I love art, I feel I chose the right major,

but I don't feel I have the luxury of becoming an artist. I should probably just learn to make a mean roast chicken with fingerling potatoes. I don't know. I hope I'm not wasting my time in this major.'

'God will use it for good, is my guess. He doesn't like to waste anything; he's thrifty as a New Englander.'

'If . . .' she said again, but didn't finish the thought. 'We'd love to have children. Four, actually.' Her cheeks colored. 'There would be geese and sheep and goats and chickens—and the children could have horses. Think of all the fertilizer for the fields and garden! Oh, and beehives, too. And there's that wonderful pond and the big creek and the woods . . . we want the whole hundred acres to be chemical-free. We know we can't save the world, but we can be kind to our hundred acres. And maybe you'd make a rope swing on the apple tree behind the house?'

Here was a veritable cornucopia of information. Clearly, Lace was the go-to on such matters of the heart.

He was grinning like a kid. 'If anything were ever enough, that should be it right there.'

'In the end, it all seems too much to contemplate. Dooley has two more years of college, then vet school, and I have three more years . . .'

She put her hand to her forehead. 'I just don't know . . . the world is so big and the opportunities so totally endless. You and Cynthia have always helped me figure things out . . .'

'Maybe it's too soon for you to try and figure things out. Know that God has a plan for your future. Watch and wait for his timing, and when it comes, you'll know.'

—Chapter 19

Father Tim tries to gather the wisdom to speak to Dooley's brother, Sammy, who just totaled Father Tim's vintage Mustang, and miraculously escaped death.

After he retired, he remembered how he had dreaded trying to fill Saturdays with something worthy, up to snuff, accountable. And now here he was, maybe for the first time, really liking this day, feeling the liberty of it, the broad possibilities.

He opened the Old Testament to Ecclesiastes, aka Solomon or Ezra, God only knows, chapter three.

> *To everything there is a season, and a time to every purpose under heaven . . . A time to weep and a time to laugh. A time to mourn and a time to dance . . . A time to be silent and a time to speak.*

It was time to speak.

—Chapter 20

'He don't even talk like Dooley n'more. It's like he's somebody else, like that stupid dirtbag dean's kid over at Bud's. What's Dooley tryin' to prove, anyhow, always thinkin' he knows it all? He don't know it all. He thinks his money makes him some kind of big shot, some kind of god? He wants a truck, he gets a truck, he wants a cue stick, he gets a cue stick,' said Sammy. 'I don't care if I live or die, it don't matter to me, I know I don't want to be like Dooley or you or Harley or nobody else, I want to be like myself.'

Come, Holy Spirit.

'I believe you're missing something here,' he said. 'You think all good things just fall into your brother's lap and are there for the taking?

'Let me tell you about Dooley. He helped raise four kids, remember? Walked you to school because there was no car to go in and no bus out that way, and nobody else to do it.

'And how about putting food on the table? He was ten years old, but he saw it as his job, and he managed that scary responsibility as best he could. Nobody starved to death, you're all still here.

'And yes, Miss Sadie provided money for his education, but do you think Dooley went off to that fine, expensive school and got by on money?

'Dooley didn't know how he was going to get by. He wanted to run away from that school, he wanted to come home where the love was. But he toughed it out with all those guys with privileged backgrounds and fast cars, who laughed at him and called him a hillbilly. He dug down deep, where most of us have to go in this life, and he found gold. He found a way to do more than just get by, he found the guts to go against all the odds and, with God's help, make something of himself.

'And maybe you think school is a piece of cake for your hotshot brother, that he just breezes through and has a good time. You would be wrong. School is hard. That's what makes it good. And because he has two more years, plus vet school, that makes it double hard—and double good. Because when he gets through, he'll have a way to help ease some of the suffering in this world.

'You brought us a kitten. You wanted it to have something to eat, a good home, a safe place. That's what Dooley wants for the animals he'll spend his life treating. A few years ago, a pony gashed its belly on a barbed-wire fence. It was dying. Dooley helped save its life. Barnabas was struck by a car and would have died, no question. But Dooley and Lace knew what to do and that good dog is still with us.

'You said that when Dooley wants a cue, he buys a cue. And he just bought a beautiful stick for you. Is this the hotshot brother who considers himself a god? Looks to me like it's a brother who's thoughtful of your needs, a brother who wants the best for you because he loves you. Actually, you've got two brothers who fit that description. Two!'

He pulled into the parking lot at the nursery and turned off the ignition.

'I hope you're listening to me, Sam.

'You're about to lose your place at Miss Pringle's because you've openly defied the few things asked of you. You'll be on the street, and for what?

'Most of your life, you've been up against it, and it looks like that's where you want to stay. You didn't have a choice when you were younger, but now you do.

'Do you want to shoot great pool or would you rather be dead?

'Do you want to build beautiful gardens or would you rather be dead?

'Do you want people to love you, really love you and care about you, or would you rather be dead and miss all that?

'You can't have it both ways.

'If you choose life, if you choose to honor yourself and others, too, I'll help you get on with it. Harley will help, Kenny will help, Cynthia, Miss Pringle, a lot of people will help.

'So you've got help—and you've got talent. And better than that, you've got God. God is on your side, Sam, because he loves you. Why does he love you, why does he love me? We can't fully understand it, but that's what God does, no matter how stupid or crazy we are, God loves us anyway. He wants the best for us, anyway. You steal my car and wreck it, I love you anyway. Do something like that again, I'll love you anyway, and I'll also do this: I'll press charges, and it won't be good.

'The party's over, Sam.'

—Chapter 20

❧ ❧

'I told you I would love to take the RV trip,' said Cynthia, 'when everything is done here.'

'What is everything? And what do you mean by done?'

She couldn't answer this; she simply didn't know; she would have to play it by ear, she said.

He switched off his bedside lamp, and prayed something best suited, in his opinion, for early morning, though indeed it was never too late in the day for these ardent petitions.

'Almighty and eternal God, so draw our hearts to you, so guide our minds, so fill our imaginations, so control our wills, that we may be wholly yours, utterly dedicated unto you, and then use us, we pray, as you will, and always to your glory and the welfare of your people, through our Lord and Savior Jesus Christ.'*

---

* *The Book of Common Prayer*

'Amen!' said his wife.

—Chapter 24

·˖⳿⸙ ⸲ ⸙⳿˖·

He took her hand and prayed their old evening prayer, as worn as the velveteen of the fabled rabbit. '. . . the busy world is hushed and the fever of life is over, and our work is done. In thy mercy, grant us a safe lodging and a holy rest and peace at the last . . .'*

'I love you,' she said.

'Love you back.'

—Chapter 27

·˖⳿⸙ ⸲ ⸙⳿˖·

Father Tim talks with Sharon McCurdy, whose husband was not happy with Father Tim's declaration of 'God Bless You' to the McCurdys' young son.

'I'll pray for you,' he said.

'Pray for me now,' she said. 'No one has ever prayed for me. Pray for my son, pray for my husband, who has Parkinson's. My God, pray for this crazy world, for the mess we're making of it.'

He switched on the kettle, and they went to the Poetry section and stood by a bookcase and he held forth his hands and she let him clasp her own.

'Lord, for the longing of Sharon McCurdy's heart and for her safety on these roads, for Professor McCurdy and the longings of his own heart, for the well-being of the bright and gifted Hastings and his

---

* *The Book of Common Prayer*

rich curiosity, and yes, Lord, for the mess we're making of your inexpressible beauty, we ask one thing: Thy will be done. Thank you for your boundless grace, for your unconditional love, for your mighty power to heal. And thank you for making yourself present to Sharon in a way she is fully able to receive with joy. Through Christ our Lord. Amen.'

She was weeping.

'When I speak of God's will, Sharon, it helps to know that he wants the best for us. If you can't believe he's there, pray anyway. If you feel he's cheap and withholding, thank him anyway. There will come a time when you'll thank him even for the hard places.'

—Chapter 29

-ᛄᢍᢋ ᠆ᠵᢋᡟ᠊

Father Tim writes to Henry Talbot, the priest who attempted suicide.

It was late, but not too late. He sat at his desk and responded to Henry Talbot's postcard.

Dear Henry,

A blessed Christmastide to you. Am grateful to know of your whereabouts—please keep in touch. Here are the few words I prayed with a searching and repentant heart:

Thank you, God, for loving me and for sending your Son to die for my sins. I sincerely repent of my sins and receive

Christ as my personal savior. Now as your child, I turn my entire life over to you.

Everything to gain and nothing to lose, my brother.

With love in Him Who loved us first,

Timothy

—Chapter 30

The angel fetched Peter out of prison, but it was prayer that fetched the angel.

—Thomas Watson

COME RAIN OR COME SHINE

Come Rain or Come Shine celebrates a wedding that thrilled fans all the way to the number one spot on the *New York Times* bestseller list. Dooley Kavanagh and Lace Harper, soul mates since childhood, finally tie the big knot. Their wedding is casual and filled with everyone's favorite Mitford characters. The icing on the cake, however, is a character readers will meet for the very first time.

He entered Meadowgate's small cemetery plot canopied by the branches of two lindens and sat on the bench.

'Lord.' He crossed himself and spoke aloud to that place beyond the fence, the fields, the blue bowl of the April sky.

'I'm here for the sundered nest, the families broken apart by anger, disappointment, violence, neglect. Thank you for your mercy and grace upon Pauline, Dooley, Kenny, Sammy, Pooh, Jessie, and all those you have associated with their lives and with their suffering. You told the farmer Joel that you would restore unto him the days the locusts had eaten. For the Barlowes and for all such families, Lord, we thank you for restoring those days to each and every one.'

—Chapter 3

Lace is preparing for the wedding.

She realized she was pacing the floor as if caged.

She was caged, in a way—by the enormity of everything, including the pressure of finishing Dooley's wedding present on time. Somehow, she needed to let it all go.

Let go and let God.

She had seen that sprayed on a wall of graffiti years ago and had written it inside the cover of her Dooley Book. She had seen it hundreds of times when opening the book, so often that she forgot to consider the meaning anymore.

She found her pen and sat in the chair by the window and opened the book in her lap.

I give my wedding dress search to you and also the weather on the 14th and the entire wedding and all the people who have worked so hard to make it happen and the people who will be coming. I give you Dooley's present and his vet practice and Choo-Choo and the girls and all the days of our wonderful life together in this beautiful place.

But most of all Lord~most of all~

I give you Jack Tyler.

—Chapter 6

Weather is always a big issue with an outdoor wedding. Here's a good way to write that concern off your list.

'Lord,' Father Tim said as he switched on the ignition, 'may it please you to give us a wonderful day with great weather. That said, Lord— and I mean this—your will be done.'

—Chapter 10

There are at least a few times in our personal history when a new person walks into our life and completely changes it. Jack Tyler, just four years old, will be given the grace to change many lives. All for the better. Let us watch carefully for those who are divinely given into our own lives, and to whom we may owe deep gratitude.

Jack Tyler was wearing a dark blue suit too large for his frame, with a dingy dress shirt and beat-up gym shoes. He carried his sole possessions in a black plastic bag with a tie—it appeared pretty empty—and held on tight to a stuffed kangaroo.

He had made it clear to the person who picked him up that he had to be called by his entire name. When people called him Jack, he felt like he was only half of himself though he couldn't have explained this feeling.

He also let the person know that he hated this stupid suit. He had never worn such a thing before, it felt like a trap. He had begged to wear his jeans and favorite T-shirt but his granny made him wear this mess.

'That is a church suit from a church sale,' said his granny. 'They're church people over there, you need to make a good impression so they'll keep you around.'

He had lived with his granny in a trailer since he was a baby and now he was four. There had been room in the yard for his trike and her truck and that was it. There had been a sandbox, but somebody had backed over it with their dirt bike. If he rode his trike across a line which he could not see but which his granny talked about all the time, the dog next door went ballistic and he ran in the trailer and hid in the bathroom and shivered all over.

'There's a toy for you under the seat,' said the person.

'I don't want a toy.'

''Cause you already have a toy, right?'

'This is not a toy, okay?' His kangaroo was his friend. Roo was more real than the person driving this smelly bad truck.

When they turned into the driveway, he got a sinking feeling like he was going to upchuck. The person got out of the truck and came around to help him down.

'No,' he said.

He jumped down with his sack, remembering what his granny said. 'Maybe I'll come see you now an' again, but things is goin' on in my life so don't look for me no time soon.'

'I won't,' he said.

This yard was big, the house was big, and this was more people than he had generally seen together at one time except when Sam Tully went off to heaven and people cried.

He wanted to cry, it felt like a cry coming, but his granny had said don't cry, you are not a baby, look at me, you don't see me cryin'. So he didn't cry, but he did think of climbing back in the truck when he saw the dogs, four of them, all barking straight at him but lying down. He had never seen a barking dog lying down.

He moved close to the person who had gone too fast around the curves. He had not said anything about going too fast but held on to his kangaroo. His granny went fast so he was used to going fast except with somebody he did not know it seemed faster.

'There's your mom and dad right there, comin' out th' door,' said the person. 'Aren't they a pretty sight! We're late as th' dickens.'

'It was th' log trucks!' the person shouted.

The mom and the dad were coming straight at him and the mom was crying even though she looked happy. He had never had a dad and could not remember anything about his real mom except the scar on her arm and the smell of her shampoo and her laugh which was really loud. He made his body stiff just in case.

The new mom squatted down to his size. 'Hey, Jack Tyler,' she said. He stepped back. She was pretty like on TV and smelled like cookies.

The new dad squatted down. 'Welcome home, Jack Tyler.'

He could see straight into their eyes.

He hardly had any breath to ask the question. 'Does those dogs go ballistic?'

'Never,' said the dad. 'They are beyond ballistic.'

'Does they bite?'

'They don't have enough teeth to bite,' said the mom.

He thought of what his granny told him. 'You're jis' bein' fostered, you ain't adopted yet so you be good, you hear?'

He thought he was pretty good except when he hated his granny so hard that he shivered and couldn't stop. He had run away once but she caught him and took his kangaroo and throwed out the baby from the pouch. She had throwed it way out in the pond and he could not swim.

When he thought of that, he could not hold it back, so he cried now and they let him do it and they cried with him and the mom said it was okay.

He thought that maybe once in a while they could do it anyway. 'Does they ever sometimes bite?'

'They don't have no teeth to bite,' said Harley. 'Like me. Looky here.' Harley made a toothless grin.

'For th' Lord's *sake*!' said Lily. 'Stop that! You'll scare 'im to death.'

He had never smelled so many good smells or seen so many people talking at the same time. On the table there was piles of cookies. Piles. He had never seen piles of cookies. And there was pies, too. A lots of pies.

'How about a sandwich with your lemonade?' said the mom.

No.

'With chicken and tomato and lettuce and mayo?'

No. He did not like to eat around strange people.

She handed him a cookie. 'It's chocolate chip,' she said. He thought her long hair was like on TV.

He took the cookie; it was still warm.

'Hey, buddy.'

It was somebody who looked like the dad but was another person with red hair. 'I'm Uncle Sammy.' Uncle Sammy was really tall and stooping down and holding out his hand. He could not shake it because he was holding his cookie.

'Welcome to th' z-zoo. We'll shoot us some pool after while,' said Uncle Sammy. 'Y-you okay with that?' he asked the mom. 'Abraham Lincoln shot pool, Mark Twain, President John Adams, V-Vanna White . . .'

She laughed. 'If there's time,' she said.

He had seen people on TV shoot pool.

'Who's your buddy there?'

'Roo.'

'He's losin' his stuffin'. I used to lose my stuffin' p-pretty regular.' Uncle Sammy laughed, rubbed him on his head just after the mom had combed his hair. 'Okay, Jack, be cool.'

'It's more than Jack,' he said. 'It's Jack Tyler.'

'Jack Tyler. G-Got it. Goin' out to see th' cattle. Catch you later.'

He had drunk a whole glass of lemonade and besides, there were so many people he had to pee. He could not wait another minute and the dad was at the barn. 'I have to go,' he said to the mom.

'Do you want to leave your kangaroo here?'

'No,' he said.

She took him by the hand and led him to what she called the hall room and shut the door and he stuffed the cookie into his mouth. He saw lights behind his eyes. He had never tasted such a good cookie. It was soft and chewy and the chocolate was runny and he had to wipe his hands on the towel.

He did what had to be done and zipped up his church pants and stood for a long time wondering when it would be okay to go back out with all those people who seemed glad to see him and what he should do to not disappoint them and keep getting cookies.

He picked up Roo, made his body stiff just in case, and opened the door.

'Jack Tyler.'

He squatted before the boy, holding back the tears. What a holy amazement. 'Welcome home. I'm Dooley's dad, Father Tim.' Maybe that was too much information.

'What's that white thing around your neck?'

'My collar. I'm a priest.' Definitely too much information. 'Have you seen the cows?'

He had wondered what to say to a four-year-old. It was a while since he'd been one.

The boy in the baggy suit was overwhelmed, as anyone would be. And he, the grown-up, had to search for words. They looked at each other for a long moment. They were both pleading for something, though he couldn't say what. Perhaps the boy was pleading for someone to trust, and himself, a priest for a half-century, pleading for a general forgiveness for not always knowing how to love. How he would get up from this squat was another matter.

'Here's a hug,' he said to Jack Tyler, who came without pretense into his arms. He held him close, feeling some of the tension flow out of the boy, out of the man, and grace flow in.

—Chapter 11

Father Tim shares a pre-wedding prayer with Dooley.

He sat with Dooley in the room off the glider porch. 'Father, we thank you from the deep place of our souls for your unending grace and mercy in Dooley's life. Thank you for patience that you may reward it, thank you for brokenness that you may mend it, thank you for love that you may enlarge it above our most heartfelt expectations.

'Thank you for working wonders in their pathway to marriage and for this exciting time of parenthood. Now teach, guide, comfort, and inspire them—as believers in the one true God, as loving husband and wife, as wise parents, and as thoughtful stewards of this good land and its many creatures. May Meadowgate always be a place where your compassion is practiced and your love freely shared.'

—Chapter 12

'Lace, do you take Dooley to be your husband; to live together in the covenant of marriage? Do you vow to love him, cherish him, honor and keep him, in sickness and in health, and forsaking all others, be faithful to him until death do you part?'

'I do.'

'Dooley, do you take Lace to be your wife; to live together in the covenant of marriage? Do you vow to love her, cherish her, honor and keep her, in sickness and in health, and forsaking all others, be faithful to her until death do you part?'

'I do.'

'Do those of you witnessing these promises vow to do all in your power to uphold Lace and Dooley in their marriage?'

'We do!'

The farm dogs slept, studied the crowd, yawned. Bowser licked himself with some vigor until Jessie gave him a shove with her foot.

'The Lord be with you!' he said to all the assembled.

'And also with you!'

'Let us pray. O gracious and ever living God, you have created us male and female in your image. Look mercifully upon Dooley and Lace, who come to you seeking your blessing, and assist them with your grace, that with true fidelity and steadfast love they may honor and keep the promises and vows they make, through Jesus Christ our Savior, who lives and reigns with you in the unity of the Holy Spirit, one God, forever and ever. Amen.'*

—Chapter 13

'Lace, you recently asked two very thoughtful questions. Is cherish the same as love? And how do we cherish someone?

'I believe cherish to be a higher plane within the context of love, something like the upstairs level in a home. Love must come first, for without it, it would be impossible to access the higher and perhaps even nobler realm of cherishing and holding dear.

'So how can we cherish another? Might there be one powerful but simple method that leads to the richness we find in the act of cherishing the beloved?

'As I studied and prayed, there it was. In Romans 12:10. A one-word marriage manual in a vigorous, no-nonsense verb.

'Outdo.

'"Outdo one another," says Paul, "in showing honor."

'What outdo means, of course, is going above and beyond. Outdo means pressed down, shaken, and running over.

'What outdo does not mean is a competition in which one person wins the game and the other loses. To outdo one another means you

---

* *The Book of Common Prayer*, The Celebration and Blessing of a Marriage

both win. In Ephesians 5:28, we're told that he who loves his wife loves himself. In effect, a good marriage happens when the happiness of the other is essential to your own happiness. We might say that a good marriage is a contest of generosities.

'How wonderful that it's possible to ensure our own happiness by seeking the happiness of another. Is it our job to make the beloved happy? It is not. The other person always has a choice. It is our job to generously outdo, no matter what, and discover that the prize in this contest of generosity is more love.

'All of which moves two outdoers in a circle, like the rings that will be exchanged today. Dooley cherishes Lace, Lace cherishes Dooley, and the circle is unbroken. It is definitely a practice of love that requires the participation of two. If only one is outdoing, that one will soon be done in.

'So we love and that is good. We cherish and that is even better.

'I would ask you to remember that you're not only husband and wife, you are also brother and sister in Christ and mother and father to Jack Tyler. Here are three opportunities to outdo without being done in, to refresh and fulfill yourselves.

'I believe many of us simply *do*. And sometimes that seems a gracious plenty. But in *out*doing, if each is giving and receiving, there's always something circling back, helping to replenish our emotional and physical strength as we help replenish theirs.

'I'll close with a very specific way to help you live the principle of outdoing. This is a key to opening hearts, a gentle pathway to cherishing your beloved. To that end, I have been given this further word.

'Listen.

'Listening is among the most generous ways to give. When a loved one talks to us—whether their words appear to be deep or shallow—listen. For in some way, they are baring their soul.

'Listen, dear Lace. Listen, my son. And you will cherish and be cherished. '

—Chapter 13

'Dooley, Lace, and Jack Tyler . . . we honor you today as a family.'

'Amen!' said the people.

'Forever.'

'Amen!'

'For better or for worse. To love and to cherish.'

'Amen!'

'Come rain or come shine!' yelled Jack Tyler, and all the people laughed and clapped.

The mom leaned down and took his left hand and put a ring on his finger and looked in his eyes really close. 'We're a family now, Jack Tyler.' She kissed him on one side of his face. 'This is forever.'

His dad squatted down and kissed him on the other side of his face and looked in his eyes and said, 'We're a family now, Jack Tyler. We'll be a family forever.'

'Those whom God has joined together let no one put asunder!' said the Granpa in a really loud voice.

—Chapter 13

Dooley's mother and her husband, Buck, two recovering alcoholics, participate in the wedding service.

The program quivered lightly in Pauline Leeper's hands. She would not weep as she was wont to do in anything associated with her children. She could, at least, do that for them.

'Give us grace when we hurt each other,' she read, 'to recognize and acknowledge our fault, and to seek each other's forgiveness and yours.

'Amen!'

She realized she had said the prayer incorrectly. It read, Give *them* grace when they hurt each other . . . and acknowledge *their* fault. She had deeply humiliated herself.

Buck Leeper did not notice his wife's revision of the prayer. He squeezed her hand as she sat down, knowing that he couldn't have made it without her. Two hopeless addicts had pushed and pulled together, mostly fifty-fifty, and by the grace of God, they had each made themselves a gift offering to the other. He knew it couldn't have happened if he hadn't prayed with Father Tim that night in the rectory. *Thank you, God, for loving me and for sending your Son to die for my sins. I sincerely repent of my sins and receive Christ as my personal savior. Now as your child, I turn my entire life over to you.* So simple. So mighty.

—Chapter 13

People who keep dogs . . . are cowards who haven't got the guts to bite people themselves.

—August Strindberg

Cat motto: no matter what you've done wrong, always try to make it look like the dog did it.

—Unknown

TO BE WHERE YOU ARE

So Father Tim has a new job, selling groceries on Main Street, while contemplating life approaching eighty. Dooley and Lace face a financial crisis that threatens their vet practice. And then comes springtime, when the prayers of three families are answered—all at once. And Dooley's biological family begins the healing process we have hoped for.

In a funeral service for Mitford's master cake baker, Father Tim reminds us that we don't have to do great things to make a difference.

'It's been estimated that everybody gets fifteen minutes of fame. Not in Esther Bolick's case. Esther enjoyed forty years of well-deserved celebrity.

'In 1977, Esther's favorite aunt died. Aunt Margaret's last will and testament gave Esther first choice of three items cherished by the deceased—a pair of diamond earrings in the shape of footballs—Aunt Margaret was a Redskins fan—a 1970 Chevelle Super Sport with bucket seats, or the recipe for her Orange Marmalade Cake.

'Esther said she struggled with this offer. She and Gene needed a car and she had always wanted a pair of diamond earrings. However, she admitted coveting since childhood the secret recipe her aunt had never shared with a living soul.

'Esther claimed her inheritance and, in a manner of speaking, ran with it.

'For forty years, spirits were lifted when people saw Esther coming with her cake carrier. For forty years she demonstrated the gold standard for generosity. For forty years, she caused everyone who received her iconic cake to feel like a million bucks. After taxes.

'I'm not saying that Esther Bolick was entirely selfless or was doing it all for others. Esther also baked the OMC for Esther—for the mystery of it, she told me. She said that every one she baked had been individual, one of a kind, just like people. Further, she enjoyed creating something beautiful and rare. But let's not overlook the possibility of an even greater payoff: I think Esther did it for the joy of seeing our everyday faces light up.

'Proverb 11:25 puts it plainly. *He that watereth shall be watered.* That simple. We got a blessing, Esther got a blessing. It was a win-win!

'All over town, people are telling their stories of Esther and the OMC. Coot Hendrick remembers the time his elderly mother was ill. It was Christmas and snowing out there on Route Four, and who showed up to deliver hope and good cheer? Esther and Gene Bolick, with chains on their tires and a two-layer OMC.

'There was the year Esther spearheaded the baking of fourteen OMCs, an endeavor that raised enough money at the Bane and

Blessing to dig a well in South Africa. Fresh, clean water in a land gone dry. A lifesaver!

'Last June, Esther baked one of our son's two wedding cakes. There was nothing left of it but a few crumbs, which, loath to waste such treasure, I raked into a Ziploc bag and hid in my coat pocket.

'Indeed, the OMC has marked more life events for me and for Mitford than we can collectively recall. But there's one event I'll never forget. This dates back to B.C., Before Cynthia, when I opened my refrigerator to find what Esther had stashed by the milk jug. An entire OMC! For a bachelor! Although this diabetic priest knew better— yes, I did—I could not resist just one . . . small . . . slice.' Many of the congregants knew what was coming.

'I woke up from a hypoglycemic hyperosmolar nonketotic coma eight days later.'

Laughter.

'It was worth it!'

More laughter, followed by applause.

'We don't have to give the world the emotional spectrum of *King Lear* or the exalted praise of the *Messiah* or the figure of David released from marble. We don't have to do great things to make a difference. We can make a difference by doing small things graciously. To that end, may we practice, as did Esther, this exhortation in Deuteronomy: *Let every man give—as he is able.* Esther gave as she was able. One cake at a time.

'Something occurred to me at the graveside. With Esther's OMC, you didn't just get cake. You got Esther. Esther delivered every cake personally. She couldn't wait to see our response to a labor of love that took four-plus hours to bring into the world.

'Indeed, creating an OMC requires a skill set of some magnitude.

'Baking the layers is easy enough. But then come the recipes for the syrup, the filling, the frosting. As for the frosting—no yogurt, no way. OMC frosting is total heavy cream, full-bore sour cream, and high-octane sugar. And how you apply the frosting will tell the world all it needs to know of your patience and good humor. After decorating the top with orange slices, you may like to present the finished product on a paper doily. The doily, Esther told me, "adds to the cost—but is required for beauty."

'Our good Winnie Ivey has honored Esther by baking the OMC Bonanza, a spectacular three-layer which is on view today at the reception. She is honoring Esther further by donating ten percent of every sale of OMC, whole or in slices, to the Children's Hospital. Thank you, Winnie Ivey, you are a treasure.

'Immediately after the reception, the ECW will lead us up the hill—in cars, thankfully—to Hope House. There we'll do what Esther would have done—deliver Winnie's three-layer to our elders, personally.

'You're invited to join us in this loving tribute to Esther, and to experience with us the joy and exuberance of giving.'

He crossed himself, bowed his head.

'Lord, we thank you for Esther's life among us. It was beautiful and rare. Thank you for all those forty years of giving that modeled your son, Jesus Christ, who walks among us still, delivering—in person—the love, grace, mercy, and forgiveness we were created to receive and enjoy.

'Amen.'

And the people said, '*Amen!*'

—Chapter 7

Avis Packard, owner of Mitford's food store, The Local, has been hospitalized with the worst of the pneumonias.

He gleaned what he could from the charge nurse.

Mr. Packard's immune system was compromised and perhaps completely shot.

Bacterial pneumonia. The really bad one.

Drips of heavy-duty antibiotics off and running.

No visitors allowed except Father Tim and one employee from the patient's place of business, all required to wear a mask and wash their hands before and after each visit.

Visits limited to five minutes. Dr. Wilson had pronounced this a law, not a suggestion.

He must not touch the patient nor tire the patient.

Upcoming tests would include X-ray of the lungs for possible damage by excessive tobacco use.

Avis's breath whistled in, whistled out as he presented his plan to the priest and concluded with an offer. 'Ten dollars an hour.'

A convulsion of coughing shook the bed.

'I don't know, Avis, I can't say right now.'

'Or fryers, roasters, chops, fresh produce. You name it, it's yours. You like a good ham . . .' Th' pain was a blowtorch in his chest, but he had to get this deal settled. 'Fresh pasta. All you need.' But who would make th' pasta? He was th' pasta man. Otis and Lisa could not make pasta. 'If I was to . . . maybe . . . you know.'

'Die?' said Father Tim. 'I don't think that's where you're headed.'

But if he did die, Avis thought, where was he headed? Up? Down? He didn't want to get into that. 'If I pass . . . maybe you could find where Chucky's at . . . an' check on him once in a while?'

'I'll do my best. Do you ever talk to God, Avis?'

'Nossir. I don't bother with God.' Wait a minute. He'd asked God for somethin' th' other day, but couldn't remember what it was.

Lungs concrete; his head mostly air. He was glad the preacher was here; he saw him through some kind of cloud. His mother had eyes the color of clouds.

She was blue an' puffed up an' wet an' layin' on th' kitchen table where she rolled out her biscuit dough, where they sat and ate their dinner.

'Why?' he asked his daddy.

'Troubled,' he said. 'She was troubled.'

People talkin' in low voices, spittin' tobacco juice in her flower beds, hammerin' in the shed, tap, tap.

'Troubled about what?' He was afraid of the answer.

His daddy shrugged an' stared out to their three head of beef cattle standin' in th' field. 'I don't know nothin' about it, boy. God only knows.' He had wondered why God seemed to know so much an' people didn't know nothin'.

'Lisa and Otis,' Avis said, 'they don't have a way with th' public. But they'll give you backup. They're hard workers. Otis'll get his daddy to come up an' butcher for us.'

'We'll figure it out.' The rattle in Avis's chest was unsettling. 'You need to rest now.'

'They can't pay th' bills or write checks or place orders.'

'It's going to work out. We'll get Marcie Guthrie to run your books. She did some work for you a while back; she'll know the ropes.'

'Lisa an' Otis can price an' shelve an' run a card an' open th' refrigerator . . . I mean th' cash drawer. As for orderin' supplies, no, an' Thanksgiving comin'.' This was a terrible thing. He could not afford to let his business go haywire with Thanksgivin' comin'. A wave of coughing churned in his chest, exploded, cracked open the concrete.

'If . . . anything . . . happens . . .' Avis forced out air to shape each word. '. . . you'll know . . . how to handle it.'

The five minutes were up. Father Tim crossed himself, prayed for words. The old petition came to mind like a bird to the outstretched palm.

'Heavenly Father, watch with us over your child Avis, and grant that he may be restored to that perfect health which is yours alone to give. Through Christ our Lord. Amen.'*

He said *amen* in the way of the Baptists, with the long *a*, as it was pronounced when he was a boy in Holly Springs. It was a simple comfort to him, a priest who felt he had little comfort to give.

—Chapter 13

By grace alone, the desperately ill Avis has convinced Father Tim to run the store in his absence.

'Good morning! Sweet Vidalia onions, five-pound bag, two-ninety-five today only. How may I help you?'

'Ahhh. Avis?'

---

* Ministration from *The Book of Common Prayer*

'Tim Kanvanagh. Avis is out for a bit.' A few weeks? A couple of months? It was daunting not to know.

'I'm a longtime fan of th' Local. Hey, I need an eight-pound beef tenderloin for tonight. I'm drivin' down from Abingdon. Is that a problem?'

'I don't know. I don't think so. Can you hold?'

'I'm ten minutes out.'

He laid the phone down, located Otis. 'Need an eight-pound beef tenderloin.'

'I can give you pork, but no beef, not today.'

Back to the phone, reporting his findings.

Sayonara to the customer who wanted beef and was now motoring to Holding's Fresh Market, forty minutes south. He should have romanced what they had, shared his no-fail pork tenderloin recipe. Avis could not afford to lose a customer. He would have to do better, think faster.

As for today's phone ad, it was good to promote what had to go out of here, but onions? He needed something to stir the imagination, lift the spirit, inspire!

Possibly something foreign. Like—Italian sausage! Store made! There you go.

'We don't have any Italian sausage,' said Otis. 'No Italian sausage.'

'Can you grind us some pork shoulder?'

'Yessir. We've got plenty in th' locker.'

'Grind us ten pounds and in an hour or two, we'll have Italian sausage.'

Otis gave him an alarmed look. 'Mild, I hope. We can't sell hot.'

'Mild, of course,' he said. 'This is Mitford. And I'll need two pounds of pork fat.'

'I can do that. But it's frozen.'

'Perfect. I'll need sugar and salt . . .'

'In th' break room.'

'And sherry. A little sherry.'

'Wine section.'

'I'll need big bowls.'

'In th' cabinet above th' sink. Avis ran his test kitchen back there.' Otis was noticeably wringing his hands over any possible bad decisions by the preacher. Sherry, pork shoulder, pork fat. These were big-money ingredients.

'How about four bucks a pound?' he asked Otis.

'Harris Teeter in Wesley gets four ninety-nine.'

'Good. Another reason to make it four bucks. But only for a limited time.' He knew something about loss leaders. Lose a little on a big item to get people in the store, right?

The only problem with this job is that he flat-out didn't know what he was doing. But he did know how to make sausage. They had made a lot of sausage at Whitefield; Peggy taught him how when he was ten years old, just before she disappeared.

He went to the spice rack. Crossed himself.

Took down the parsley, the garlic powder, the fennel seeds, the cracked pepper . . .

—Chapter 13

She had her coffee, he had his tea; they had their Advent reading.

Although the Lord gives you the bread of adversity and the water of affliction, your teachers will be hidden no more; with your own eyes you

*will see them. Whether you turn to the right or to the left, your ears will
hear a voice behind you saying, 'This is the way; walk you in it.'*

—Isaiah 30:20–21

—Chapter 17

Family gathers at Meadowgate Farm to celebrate Jack Tyler's
Name Day ceremony.

Everyone processed from the kitchen to the living room. Beth and
Tommy up front, leading the singing to Henry Van Dyke's hymn of joy.

Next were Dooley, Lace and Jack, then Hoppy, Olivia, Cynthia, Pauline and Buck. After Pauline and Buck, Sammy, Kenny,
Julie, Etta, Ethan, Pooh, Rebecca Jane, Doc Owen, Marge Owen,
Blake, Amanda, Harley, Willie, Lily, Violet, and bringing up the
rear, the priest, vested for the occasion in Advent color. He could
have worn jeans and a collar, sure, but Jack liked vestments!

Beth and Tommy took their places with four band members who
were grouped beneath the stairwell.

The congregation, each clutching a program, seated themselves
in the Crossroads folding chairs. Jack in boots, new corduroys,
checked shirt, navy blazer, and his first tie, sat between his mom and
dad on the front row.

The service would be brief, informal, and simple. The family
baptism ceremony in July had been properly ceremonious, but, rea-
soned the celebrant, far too long for a four-year-old.

Father Tim stood before them and signed the cross.

'Blessed be God: Father, Son, and Holy Spirit.'

'And blessed be his kingdom, now and forever. Amen!'

Acknowledgments

With very special thanks to Ivan Held, publisher and friend.

And to Danielle Dieterich for her vision and resourcefulness.

Many gratitudes, also, for the heartfelt contributions of Christine Ball, Sally Kim, Ashley McClay, Emily Ollis, Jordan Aaronson, Alexis Welby, Katie McKee, Madeline Schmitz, Elena Hershey, Meredith Dros, Maija Baldauf, Linda Rosenberg, Claire Sullivan, Marie Finamore, Anthony Ramondo, Monica Cordova, and Lynn Buckley.

With special thanks to John MacDonough, who has been the one true voice of Mitford to his legions of loving fans. John, you made Mitford seem real. Which, of course, it is. We love you.

'Into your hands, O God, we place your child, Jack Brady Kavanagh. Thank you for supporting him in his successes and his failures, in his joys and in his sorrows. May he grow in grace and in the knowledge of our Savior Jesus Christ. Amen.'

'*Amen!*'

'Jack, may he bless you with his peace and keep you in plenty all the days of your life, that you might bring forth much fruit in his kingdom. Brothers and sisters, I present to you, Jack Brady *Kavanagh*!'

Applause. Tears. Laughter.

Tommy stood and strummed his guitar.

'Here are the chords,' said Tommy. 'Short an' easy, okay? Here they are again. The words are in your program. Clap twice where it says to, an' everybody sing big.

'*Jack, Jack, we've got your back!*'

Clap, clap. '*Jack Kavanagh!*'

'Again!'

'*Jack, Jack, we've got your back!*'

Clap, clap. '*Jack Kavanagh!*'

Applause. Whistles. Jack laughing.

'That was fun,' said Father Tim. 'You know who else has your back?'

'Charley!'

Charley barked. More laughter.

'Jesus!' said Father Tim. 'Love him and trust him, for he will always be there for you.'

Jack tugged on his granpa's chasuble. 'I have a great idea, Granpa Tim! You an' Jesus could make my fake cousin an' fake aunts an' uncles be real!'

'Well, now, that is truly a great idea.' He took Jack's hand. 'We're going to have to pray again, everybody! As St. Paul instructed us in Colossians, Be *instant* in prayer!

'Father, please help us all to be real with Jack and with one another. Help us to seek a true kinship of the heart, always. Through Christ our Lord. Amen!'

'*Amen!*'

Father Tim produced a small box from beneath his chasuble.

'We have something special for you today. It's from Granny Pauline, Granny Olivia, Granny Cynthia, Granpa Buck, Granpa Hoppy, and myself.'

'I have a *ton* of grannies and granpas!'

Laughter, applause.

He opened the lid of the box and showed the contents to Jack.

'A watch!'

'Take it out and look at the back. See your new name? With today's date? Let me help you latch it. Good fit, with room to grow! There, now. What time is it?'

Jack stared hard at the watch face. He wanted to get this perfect.

'Twenty . . . one . . . *minutes after twelve*!' he yelled. Charley barked. All applauded.

Father Tim laughed. 'But wait!' he said. 'There's more!'

To the clonking of a cowbell wielded by Rebecca Jane, up the hall rolled the red bike, Lace holding one handlebar, Dooley the other.

Just for the heck of it, Father Tim timed the jubilation. Four minutes plus change, which could have gone on till the cows came home again, but he brought it to order with Jack at his side.

'Lunch is scheduled for twelve-thirty,' said Father Tim. 'And Jack has a message for us.'

'*Twenty-six minutes after twelve!*' yelled Jack.

'Time is always ticking away. May we choose, every moment, to love one another as God loves us. Go in peace, now, to love and serve the Lord.'

'*Thanks be to God!*'

The Biscuits played. Tommy and Beth sang an old Sunday school standard.

> '*Jesus loves the little children,*
> *All the children of the world,*
> *Red and yellow, black and white,*
> *They are precious in His sight . . .*'

Everyone scrambled toward the kitchen; toward the turkey, the ham, the fire on the hearth, the tables with a place set for Miss Sadie . . .

And Jack yelled at the top of his lungs. '*Thirty minutes after twelve!*'

—Chapter 20

Occasioned by a phone call that was a wrong number, Father Tim counsels defense attorney Brooke Logan as to the vital, albeit unpopular role of surrender in our relationship with God.

'In nearly five decades of working with human souls, I've seen how we can define ourselves by how we've been wounded. In every way, unforgiveness makes us the victim—nothing that a defense attorney would wish to be, I'm sure.

'Surrender is the key that unlocks the hard heart and gives love the liberty to enter. Where love enters, the possibilities for forgiveness go viral.'

'I don't surrender, Father. I really don't. I think we need to end this conversation, it's not going anywhere for me.'

'May I give you a few words more? By someone far wiser than either of us?'

'If you must.' Snappish.

'Blaise Pascal was a brilliant mathematician, inventor, philosopher. *There is a God-shaped vacuum in the heart of every person,* he said, *and it cannot be filled by any created thing. It can only be filled by God, made known through Jesus Christ.*

'At the age of forty, I was a priest who believed with the intellect, but knew nothing of the intimacy with God that comes with surrender. I was certifiably lost—holding on to my pain, trying to fill the God-shaped vacuum. Then one day, standing in the backyard of the rectory, I was moved to pray a simple prayer from the heart. I surrendered everything. And everything changed.'

She laughed. 'So there's a trick prayer that solves all our problems? You would be a poor candidate for the witness stand.'

'It has power to do what's intended.'

'What exactly is its intent?'

'To lead us out of ourselves. Liberate us from the gridlock of ego.'

'The gridlock of ego. You sound like my husband. Okay, you've been kind to listen to me. What is the prayer?'

'Thank you, God, for loving me and for sending your son to die for my sins. I repent of my sins and receive Christ as my savior. And now, as your child, I surrender my entire life to you.'

Long silence, and then laughter. 'Oh, no. I'm not ready for that, not at all, no. It's not *my* sins I'm calling about, Father. Or perhaps you have misunderstood.'

They were both exhausted.

'Call me anytime,' he said. 'If I don't answer, you may get my deacon, Cynthia, who just happens to be my wife. She's wonderful. You'll love her, everybody does. She was betrayed, too, you see, and really gets it.'

He sat for a time after they said their goodbyes.

A few nights ago, Cynthia mentioned that she was ready for him to retire, once and for all.

But no. Old priests never retire; they just get the occasional wrong number.

—Chapter 21

The Lord is my strength and my shield; my heart trusts in Him and I am helped; therefore my heart greatly rejoices; and with my song will I praise him.

—Psalm 28:7

Acknowledgments

With very special thanks to Ivan Held, publisher and friend.

And to Danielle Dieterich for her vision and resourcefulness.

Many gratitudes, also, for the heartfelt contributions of Christine Ball, Sally Kim, Ashley McClay, Emily Ollis, Jordan Aaronson, Alexis Welby, Katie McKee, Madeline Schmitz, Elena Hershey, Meredith Dros, Maija Baldauf, Linda Rosenberg, Claire Sullivan, Marie Finamore, Anthony Ramondo, Monica Cordova, and Lynn Buckley.

Jan Karon is the #1 *New York Times*–bestselling author of fourteen novels in the Mitford series, featuring Episcopal priest Father Tim Kavanagh. She has authored twelve other books, including *Jan Karon's Mitford Cookbook and Kitchen Reader*, and several titles for children. Jan lives in Virginia near the World Heritage site of Jefferson's Monticello.